The Life and Times of William Boule

Max China

First Published by skinnybirdproductions: 31 July 2014

Copyright © 2014 Max China
All rights reserved
ISBN: 978-0-9571-3128-6 Paperback

For my children, Charlotte and Sam

ACKNOWLEDGEMENTS

I'd like to thank everyone who has contributed to the process of producing this book, with special thanks to Chloe McDonald, talented author of *The Trilogy of Noor*, for her much-valued advice, continuing encouragement and for sketching the police artist's impression of William Boule, which features on the front cover of this book. I'm extremely grateful...

Close your eyes. Can you still see?

Prologue

November 2007

The fact the package came by courier was nothing out of the ordinary, but my stomach churned when I saw the solicitor's name and address on the back.

My heart beat a crazy rhythm as I opened the brief letter accompanying Carla's book, and then sank as I read the note:

Dear Mr Mailer

We understand you were party to an agreement with our client, Ms Carla Black, to publish her work in your newspaper if she failed to appear in person at our offices by a designated date. In accordance with her wishes, we hereby enclose a copy of her book ...

I stopped reading. My mind drifted back to the last time I'd seen her. We'd met for dinner in an expensive restaurant. She hardly ate anything while she outlined her plans.

'I've written a book, and I've done it with the sole intention of baiting a serial killer into coming after me.'

'OK ...' I said, 'but why would you want to do that?'

'Because if I can get him to come after me to England and then get him arrested, it'll be a big story.'

'Sounds dangerous. Does this killer have a name?'

She laughed. 'Of course. It's William Boyle. Do you remember that manhunt a few months ago? Well, I'm pretty sure I know where he is, and I have it on good authority that he's calling himself by his old Foreign Legion name, William Boule.'

'I remember that story. We ran it for a few days until our sources dried up. How did you find out about his Legion name?'

She tapped her nose with a well-manicured forefinger. 'I can't tell you exactly, but let's just say I tracked someone down who confided in me.'

I nodded. 'So he's somewhere out of the country, you've already said as much, but what makes you think he'll come after you?'

'I've had a limited run of books printed, with an artist's impression of what he looks like on the front cover. Posters too. I'm going to go and put them up in the town I think he's holed up in. If he's there and he sees the book's for sale, he'll buy a copy. If he does, if he reads what I've said about him, from what I've learned, it'll send him into a rage and he'll come for sure.'

I shook my head. 'You should go to the police, Carla.'

She arched an eyebrow, looking faintly amused. 'And ruin my story? I think not.'

'You won't *have* a story if he gets to you.'

'He won't, not if it all goes to plan.'

'Why are you telling me all this, Carla?'

'I want you to promise to run a serialization of the story, come what may.'

'I can't do that. I haven't seen it yet.'

She smiled seductively. 'I think you can. This is what I propose: If I don't show up at my solicitors by, say, the end of the month, they'll send you a copy of the book. All the necessary documentation has been drawn up – all you have to do is sign. You're really going to have to trust me on this,' she said, picking up her fork. She twisted it into her food, and then laid it down again. 'Well, what do you think?'

'It's too dangerous, that's what I think.'

'But David, what a story it'll be … and besides, I'll be in and out of there in no time, and well gone by the time he buys the book. I'm sure I don't have to tell you that I'm trusting you not to tell anyone what I've told you. I leave for Essaouira in Morocco the day after tomorrow.'

I'd tried to talk her out of it, but I should have known better. She was as hard-nosed as she was headstrong, just as her father had been reputed to be; she'd have none of it. Instead, she passed me a card with her solicitor's details on it.

Her last words echoed in my head. *'Don't worry, you won't hear from them ...'*

That book, *The Life and Times of William Boule,* sat on my desk like the harbinger of doom.

It wouldn't have been sent if she were still alive.

At last, I summoned up the courage to pick up the book and flick through it.

There was no narrative story as such; it read more like reportage, simply outlining the opinions of people she'd met or tracked down who were willing to talk.

I started to read, making notes for the serialization, in order to keep my side of the bargain.

David Mailer, Editor, *Daily Times*

Chapter 1

There was something not right about William. They say the madness took him as soon as he was old enough to understand he was different. Oh, he loved his mother dearly all right – God rest her soul – but he cursed his parents.

Y'see, they'd passed on the hare's curse to him – y'know what I'm saying? Look, the women ... if they catch sight of the hare while pregnant, the child they're carrying will have the animal's lips when it's born, and he got it double, see. Worse than either of them ...

Kept himself to himself, that one. A real dark horse. Never knew what he was thinking. That stutter of his, when he was a boy, got him bullied something terrible ... the other kids, see. But he never complained; never hardly said a word. Let his fists do the talking, and all that standing up for himself ... he learned to fight. Wasn't long before the other kids learned to leave him alone.

When he was about, oh, eleven years old, you'd often hear him arguing with someone – even when we knew he was on his own – or he'd cry out in the dead of night. People complained, but not to them, to me. They was afraid, see.

We had to keep him and his ma well away from everyone else in the camp.

Aye, there was something not right about that boy.

Archie Brooks, Gypsy elder and former neighbour

Southern Morocco, October 2007 – outside temperature 43 degrees Celsius

Sensitive to the tiniest vibrations, a lizard scurried clear of the road's baking surface a full ten seconds before a white truck rattled over its former basking place.

Travelling at speed, the vehicle drew clouds of dust into the vortex trailing behind.

The road ahead shimmered. For as long as he could remember it had been like this – hours of driving through rocky, half-barren hilly wasteland, mile after mile of desert. The rolling dunes at times resembled the contours of a voluptuous woman, laid out naked, soaking up the relentless sun beating down from brilliant blue skies which darkened to azure along the horizon, and high, high in the air, hanging always just beyond his line of sight, dogging him – a bird of prey.

A yellow light glowed faintly next to the fuel gauge. *Shit. Almost empty.*

In the shade of a group of olive trees at the edge of the garage forecourt, a middle-aged Moroccan dozed, leaning back, legs sprawled out, sandalled feet resting on a knee-high flat boulder. A small herd of nearby goats bleated, alerted by something. The man drew his legs in and allowed the chair to return all four of its feet to the ground. He raised the edge of the wide-brimmed leather cowboy hat, and squinted into the distance with hawkish eyes.

From his vantage point he could see the horizon in both directions – the road out into the desert and the other way, into the nearest town. Here, he would catch those running on empty or not wanting to chance making it to the bigger and cheaper gas stations, and those who decided to top up before the long journey out across the desert, since the sign suggested – falsely – that his was the last petrol for over two hundred kilometres.

A distant cloud of dust framed the glimmering waters of a mirage in the road, and seconds later a white vehicle emerged as if crossing through a portal from another dimension. He stood up on creaking limbs, stretched and prepared himself at the roadside, ready to wave the driver in.

A black-clad figure stepped out from the dirty-white, single-storey adobe building behind. Lush black hair swept across her forehead, framing her face, before disappearing into the neck of her tunic.

A girlish voice enquired hopefully, 'A customer?'

'Go back inside, Sufiya,' he hissed at his daughter, 'and cover yourself.'

Miller's eyes snapped open. He'd had this kind of dream before, only this time it reminded him of a fleeting thought that had crossed his mind while driving home the previous day.

He rolled out of bed as stealthily as possible, careful not to wake Stella.

Picking his telephone up from the bedside table, he padded naked from the room.

'Where are you going?' Stella croaked, her throat full of sleep.

'I have to make a call.'

'What time is it?'

'Three a.m.'

'What?'

'Go back to sleep.'

The telephone cranked through different exchanges until, finally, an unfamiliar dialling tone reached his ear. *She's abroad.*

Carla snatched the phone up, irritated at the disturbance but mellowing when she saw who was calling. *Must be important.*

'Miller, do you have any idea what the time is?'

'Where are you?' he said.

'It doesn't matter. Why are you calling me at this ungodly hour?'

'I had a dream about him, Carla. I dreamed Boyle found your book, and now he's coming for you.'

'Oh, shit,' she said.

'What do you mean, oh, shit?'

'I'm in a little place in southern Morocco with a suitcase full of books and posters, hawking around shops or anywhere else that'll display them ...'

'Carla?'

'What?'

'You'd better get back here. If he finds you ...'

'I *want* him to find me.'

'But not over there ... Come home.'

She paused, and then said, 'Come and get me.'

The telephone clicked, and she was gone. Miller looked at the disconnected handset. *Why does she always have to be so difficult?*

Stella sidled up next to him, still warm from bed. He wrapped his arm around her, drawing her closer.

'Was that Carla?'

He nodded.

Her eyes dulled, and she moved almost imperceptibly, allowing a space to grow between them. 'What's going on?'

'I had a vision this morning ... I suddenly realized I'd had that kind of view before. I don't know why, but I never recognize these things first time out ...'

'What are you talking about? You told me those things don't happen to you anymore.'

'It's the first time in months. Yesterday, I saw something in my mind's eye. I thought it was just a daydream, but then – just now – I realized *exactly* what it was.'

'I'm not being funny, but what does that have to do with Carla?' she said. 'Maybe it *was* just a dream.'

'Oh, Stella ...' He took her hand and kissed her fingertips. 'I wish it was just a dream and nothing to do with her. That's why I phoned – to make sure it wasn't. But it is.' He sighed. 'She's gone to Morocco looking for Boyle, trying to draw him out of the woodwork. I thought he might have just crawled away and died after what happened with you and Eilise, but he hasn't. I saw him ... and he isn't far from Carla ...'

'Call the police; let them deal with it,' she said evenly.

'It's more complicated than that. First they'd have to find him. They'd have to do that before he gets to her. I'm beginning to think she'd do anything to nail a story. She's fearless, too much so for her own good ...'

Stella bit into her lower lip. 'She's always going to lure you in, isn't she?'

'I can't just leave her. Maybe, if I help her this one last time, we'll get rid of Boyle once and for all, and I know you'd like that, Stella, wouldn't you?'

'I'm coming with you,' she said.

He smiled and rolled his eyes heavenward, too tired to argue.

She moulded herself against him, pressing for an advantage to quash resistance, and her lips brushed his neck below the ear as she whispered, 'Come back to bed.'

Chapter 2

It was hard to find anyone on the travellers' site, where he grew up, willing to talk about him. The general consensus seemed to be: what if he comes back and finds out we said something? I did, however, manage to persuade a few with the promise of anonymity. From those conversations, another picture began to emerge. Boyle's disadvantages had made him determined to compensate. According to one woman, he'd disappear with her into remote places taking with him books and plays which he'd read aloud, acting out the different roles, experimenting with his voice. She told me he listened to tapes of famous speeches; he learned to speak just like Churchill, his voice indistinguishable. He could imitate Richard Burton, or anybody he set his mind to. She also said that while he was role-playing, he never stuttered at all.

 I found that really interesting.

Carla Black

Soon as he could, 'cos of the lip, he grew himself a moustache. What with that and he couldn't talk properly, gave him a big complex. I ain't makin' excuses for him, mind, I think he'd have been an arsehole anyway. Didn't have no idea how to talk to people. No fuckin' manners at all. I never met anyone who'd had more than two words out of him. Most thought he wasn't capable of it, but I thought it was all an act. He wasn't stable, y'know. He was unpredictable like y'wouldn't believe. Y'never knew where y'were with him, but it kept people away, and I think that was how he liked it.

Anonymous source

The battered white Toyota pick-up pulled in beside the only pump. The station owner, having used his hat to wave the driver in, replaced it on his head and then grinned, revealing that most of his teeth were missing.

Undoing the fuel cap and inserting the pump nozzle into the mouth of the tank, he began to fill it. Most people, going into town, wanted just enough to make it to the bigger stations, where they could fill up for much less. The driver didn't tell him how much to put in. He would fill it to the top unless told otherwise. The extortionate rates he charged meant he'd make a good profit – if he could only distract the driver's attention for long enough ...

His eyes flicked over the truck. The scraped bodywork was covered in dents; it looked like it had come from Beirut, though it bore a French number plate.

'*Francais*?' he enquired, raising an eyebrow.

The driver's eyes narrowed. He nodded.

'Come far?'

'France,' he said, and pointed to the man's hat. 'I want that. How much?'

'No ... no sale.' He shook his head emphatically.

'OK,' he said, scouring the dilapidated forecourt, taking in everything he saw. He took a cigarette from his top pocket, sliding it out without removing the pack or taking his eyes from the man before him. 'You got anywhere I can freshen up?'

The older man shook his head uneasily, and pointed to a sign. *Ne fumez pas.*

The stranger caught a shift in the shadows behind the glass of the improvised shop front, which was little more than a glorified home conversion. Whatever he'd seen was black and formless, but he knew what that meant. Looking at the Muslim equivalent of a hillbilly in front of him, he winced at the thought. *Some old hag.*

The other man replaced the nozzle in its holster.

'One thousand fifty dirham,' he said, holding out his hand, attempting to charge almost double.

Silence hung between them. Acutely aware of the difference in size between them, the Moroccan moved his left hand beneath his robe with a casualness that seemed to indicate he was merely scratching himself beneath it.

The big man pulled a wallet stuffed with notes from his pocket. 'Inside, I pay inside,' he said, grinning. 'Maybe you've got something for me in there – water, beer ... I pay good price.'

Licking his lips nervously, for a reason he couldn't specify, he scooted ahead, babbling in Arabic, confident the stranger would not understand. He was an Englishman; there was no disguising that – at most he may have had a little French. The Moroccan sneered disdainfully and backed in through the door, half-turning and hissing a command at the figure inside. The beads at the rear of the shop parted, swinging together again as the black-clad figure in full burqa disappeared into the gloom the other side.

Behind him, the scratch and popping flare of a match told him the man had moved in close. *Too close.* He swivelled round to protest at the smoking, but his voice was snared, choked off by a huge hand that struck at his throat with the speed of a mamba, the other clamping his wrist beneath his clothes, allowing him no time to draw his dagger. He flailed ineffectively, feet scrabbling for purchase on the floor, trying to break the choking grip that crushed his larynx, desperately hoping his daughter would hear the sound of the struggle and flee.

The stranger hoisted him higher and throttled him.

A door creaked open at the rear of the shop. He let his victim drop, lifeless, unfolding in directions he would have found impossible if he were still alive. Stepping across the body, the killer strode rapidly through the shop, and out through the back door.

The hag!

Clad head to foot in black, she ran as fast as the robe would allow.

That's no old boiler under that get-up! Too quick, too agile ... He started forward, slowly attaining a sprint; he caught her easily, and threw her to the ground. *Why didn't she scream?* He realized no one would have heard. He smiled, unbuckled his trousers, and pulled off her burqa. *A mystery bag ... and what a lovely surprise!* He moistened his lips and tore off the rest of her clothes.

When he'd finished, he gathered her garments and swooped, heaving her body up over his shoulder. He then set about the business of concealing her and the man inside the shop. Filling a bucket with petrol, he poured the contents over the two of them. 'That'll teach you to try to rip me off,' he muttered. By the doorway, he stooped and picked up the attendant's leather hat, trying it for size. It fitted. Striking a match, he flicked it inside and, turning away, the boom and whoosh of heat scorched his back as he ambled back to the truck.

Moroccan women ... I forgot what I'd been missing.

He turned the key in the ignition, and the engine sputtered into life. He floored the accelerator and, wheels screeching, headed into town.

Chapter 3

William Shaw – that was the da's name, but we all called him Bronco Billy. No good, drunken womanizer he was. Given to disappearing acts, especially when he owed money. Once, he went out for cigarettes – never came back for a year.

The ma, left to bring the boy up on her own, tried making him decent. The old man called him Billy-boy, but her and her sisters called the lad by his middle name, Martin. As he grew older, she realized that her son had more of his da's ways than hers.

When he was seventeen she died and, with her passing, all hope for the boy went too. After the funeral, he took to calling himself Boyle, after his ma's maiden name, but not before he fell out with the old man. They say he ran Bronco off the camp and, just to be sure he never came back, he burned down the family home.

Eventually, Boyle showed his face again, challenged me for the bare-knuckle championship and took it from me. Then, just like his da, he disappeared for ten years.

So far as I know, no one ever saw Bronco Billy again.

Archie Brooks

Essaouira, Morocco

Carla stepped out from the hotel into the sunlight, squinting across the car park. She put on her sunglasses.

Although the suitcase was on wheels and weighed only half what it did the day before, Carla found the effort of dragging it around in the heat exhausting. The posters weren't a problem; she paid a group of street kids to put them up all over the town in prominent positions, giving them half the money upfront with the promise of the balance when she had seen them all posted.

After a short walk through the gardens she exited through a black, intricately-worked iron gate and had barely left the shadow of the hotel when she heard the hollow thud of a foot connecting with a football. She swivelled in the direction of the sound in time to see the spinning black and white orb slicing through the air, followed by a shout of 'Mo!'

Mo moved half a pace and squared his chest, intercepting the ball. It dropped at his feet. The other boys surged towards him. He stood motionless, impassive, one foot resting on top of the ball – but only for a split second – before darting left, then right, twisting between the other boys – past two, then three – the ball controlled as if linked invisibly to his feet. Switching from one foot to the other, he made it all the way through his opponents, and then stopped abruptly. Turning, he echoed the stance he'd started with and, as the boys rushed him once more, he dazzled them as he wove through the bodies and feet that sought to dispossess him of the ball.

Carla watched him. *He's good. Very good.*

Then he saw her. 'All posters up, lady,' he said as he approached, holding out his hand. 'My part of our bargain is finished, now it is your turn, *non*?'

'Wait, when I see them all posted ... that was the deal.'

'I have put all up in the Medina, we will walk to see.'

'Mohammed,' she sighed, 'it's too hot. I'm going to have to trust you, but what about the rest, outside the traffic-free zone?'

'OK, is no problem, I call my father for show you the rest.'

'No, really, I don't have time ...'

Despite her protests, Mohammed called him. 'He is taxi driver, lady, he take you, you will see. Come,' he said, taking over the towing of the suitcase. 'We walk to meet him.'

The taxi arrived within minutes, and the boy quickly loaded the case into the boot and coerced her into the car. They took off on a wild ride around the town as he rattled off facts and figures like a fledgling tour guide, directing his father to where he'd put the posters, to prove they were in place.

Carla took in the architecture. Most of the buildings were dirty-white, occasionally buff or terracotta. Nearly all had doors and shutters painted an intense shade of blue. Arches of every description stood out in relief from the stucco. Decorative ironwork, twisted and scrolled, almost delicate, belied its primary function of securing openings against intrusion. The further from the Medina they travelled the more modern the dwellings became, and the less vibrant the atmosphere as the crowds thinned. *I'll never get used to those blue Coca-Cola awnings.*

Mohammed interrupted her musings, pointing at one of the posters stuck to a red ochre wall. 'What for you put these up?' Sweat stood out in tiny beads on his forehead.

She wiped her brow, relieved she wasn't perspiring as much as he was. 'I'm distributing a book I wrote,' she said and, seeing him struggle with the longest word, rephrased it. 'In my bag, I have books from the poster. I give to shops to sell for me.'

'*I* sell for you,' he announced proudly.

'No, Mohammed, it's something called sale or return.' She knew she'd probably have to sweeten many deals, the same as the day before, with a retainer to persuade the owners to stock them, initially two per shop. 'Only I can do it.'

After she'd been returned to the Medina and she'd paid for her trip, the boy, ever looking to expand his enterprise, offered to help her distribute the contents of the suitcase by towing it round for her. She was wishing she'd taken him up on the offer, but then thought about his incessant chatter and was glad she'd promised him a retainer to be paid each morning to stay away. 'But keep an eye out for me,' she said, softening the rejection with a smile.

His small white teeth flashed as he grinned, and deep laughter lines formed in the otherwise smooth skin at the corners of his eyes. 'Beautiful lady,' he said, looking most sincere. 'This I do. For me, I want nothing … for my brothers and sisters; I do for very small price.'

'Thank you, Mohammed,' she said, counting out and paying him the money she owed, adding a small amount on top.

He stood watching her as she hauled the case into the first randomly selected shop of the day.

By noon, she was perspiring freely. People were complaining of the unusual heat so late in the year. She wiped her face and hands with a moist tissue she took out of a sachet, and sprayed herself with a little cologne. The last shop had a spinning rack outside, packed full with books. Taking two from the display, she went inside to pay. By the time she left, two of her own books had replaced them in the revolving stand. She wondered how long it would take Boyle – if he were there – to see the posters and seek out the book.

It was the poster that caught his eye first, and then her photograph. With a very long memory, and the ability to recall the smallest detail at will, he knew who she was straight away. The flyer displayed the title: *The Life and Times of William Boule.*

He shook his head at the image. *That don't look like me, but she's used your old Foreign Legion name ... how did she find that out?* He wanted to scream, to vent his fury. He growled low in his chest and reached for the bottom edge, which had come unstuck. About to rip it down, he glanced over his shoulder. There were too many people around to display his anger immediately. He calmed himself. *Why would she write a book about me?* He considered the question further. *I'll not have her trying to make a profit out of me.*

Across the dusty street, he noticed a store with a rack of books on display. This close to the poster, the shop would surely have a copy. Lighting a cigarette, he drew hard and deep; the end glowed orange, turning a pale, acetylene yellow inside and, sucking in another huge draw, he stomped over the road to the shop.

He recognized the miniature poster image from twenty yards away. With two copies facing outwards in the rack, he couldn't miss them. Underneath the awning, somewhat shaded, his eyes took a moment to adjust. He couldn't see anyone looking, but he felt the stare of someone watching from the shadows. For a brief moment he considered stealing the book, but then decided against it. The leather Stetson felt tight. Either it had shrunk, or his head had swelled in the heat. *That little bitch fucked your head up good and proper.* 'And you don't think I know that? Stay out of my face!' he snapped, grimacing. Taking the book from the rack, he went inside.

In the shop's relative gloom, he made out the outline of two people. His eyes adjusted. One was a police officer. Both men regarded him coolly, continuing their conversation as he held out the book. The officer's gaze scoured his face, taking in his Colonel Custer moustache, and broken features. Nothing was said throughout long-stretched seconds while the shopkeeper took the book, put it into a bag, and announced the price. Without taking his eyes from the officer, he reached into his pocket and placed a handful of money on the counter. 'Enough?' he said.

'You,' the policeman said, 'you *pugiliste*?'

He drew his fist up and held it at his chin in a classic boxer's pose. 'Yes,' he said, adding, 'I was ... once.'

Leaning forwards to inspect the tattooed knuckles the other man read them aloud, hesitant as he enunciated each letter, spelling out the word. 'W-R-A-T-H,' he said. 'Your name?'

'*Oui*,' he agreed and, taking his change, left the store.

Further down the street, on his way back to the hotel, he spotted a pair of elaborately embossed, down-at-heel cowboy boots with a price tag on them, outside a bric-a-brac shop.

Minutes later he was clomping down the street, kicking up dust. With his new footwear, leather Stetson, jeans and lumberjack-style shirt, Custer moustache and long yellow hair, he looked like an outlaw on the run.

Back in his room at a rundown hotel, he flopped down onto the bed without removing any of his clothes. Stretching to his full length, he caught a whiff of his own stale sweat. He'd share that with someone later. He loved to share. A grin stretched his lips and pulled painfully on his harelip scar. He removed the book from its packaging and folded the outer cover back on itself.

Opening the first page, he read what Brooks had said about him. *Is that fuckin' so, Archie? We'll see who's right or not soon enough.* As he turned the page a waft of perfume found his olfactory senses and stimulated thoughts in him. He imagined it was the author's perfume, but it couldn't be. More than likely it was the whiff of a rich German tourist; they got in everywhere, and he'd met one or two, albeit briefly. No, it wasn't the scent of a German woman; he found no connections there. He sniffed again.

The fragrance was fresh. *Today's?* Maybe even from just a couple of hours ago. He toyed with himself, focusing on the journalist's photo; tantalizing scents coming from the book's edges aroused him, driving him almost crazy. He licked the glossy image of her face. The tang of perfume spread over his tongue, setting fire to his loins. Then he froze.

Why the fuck is a book about me being marketed in this flyblown place? He put it down, swung his legs off the bed and walked to the window, opening it. The sounds outside mingled with the dust and choking traffic fumes. A whole host of other smells came through, joining the assault on his senses. Lighting a cigarette, he blew a dense plume of smoke with enough force to project it some two and a half feet out, before it was taken upwards and away from the building by warmer currents of air. 'Does she know you're here, Willy boy?' he said, and then, flicking the cigarette end outwards, hard enough to shower sparks, he grabbed his keys and left the room. He drove to the next town along ... to see how many posters of him had been put up there.

Coming this far south reminded him of how he had once visited the sites of some of the old forts the Foreign Legion had abandoned. Not normally one for history, he had absorbed some of the fighting spirit of those men who'd gone before, fought to the last drop ... The visits helped him in some way when he returned to England. His mother had said the only influences he'd come back with were those of the criminal element. He'd scoffed at her. Some of them were the bravest men anyone could meet. *They didn't care, see, Mum, they had nothing to lose.*

Arriving in Ghazoua, he looked out for the posters. There were none. His instincts told him he there wouldn't be any more, anywhere else.

Whoever had put them up knew he was in Essaouira, and they were nothing to do with Interpol.

He grinned wolfishly. *She's still here.*

Chapter 4

Always a cautious man, he returned to his room, collected his meagre belongings and checked out from where he was staying.

After a short drive he rented a room in another fleapit on the outskirts of Mogador. Dumping his kitbag on the stained carpet, he reclined on the bed with the book, and delicately traced the full lips on the back-cover photograph with the tip of his finger. A faraway memory sprang into life ... the passing of a video tape to her, outside the offices of a Sunday newspaper well known for its salacious and scandalous articles.

Back then, she had no part to play in his plans other than drawing attention to an identity he was about to leave behind. His mind wandered through various abduction scenarios. He would see her at a busy market and trail her down the quieter streets as she browsed. Clothes and jewellery – that's what she'd be into, he decided. His fantasy shifted. In it, he ran a stall and sat in the shade with his legs stretched out, feet tucked into his newly acquired cowboy boots. He'd watch her from under the brim of his hat as she held up a range of fine cotton dresses.

'Can I try this one?' she'd ask, and he'd direct her into the back of his walk-in transporter van. Closing the rear doors for her privacy, she'd start stripping off, and he'd watch for a bit through a secret spyhole. Then, after silently locking the back doors, he'd jump in and drive her off somewhere.

He'd make her love him, just as he had Kathy.

Kathy. He hadn't meant to think of Kathy. She was gone; he knew that. Those people would have got inside her head and turned her against him. With all the precision his videographic memory allowed, he recalled how he'd taken her that night. She was so stoned it was easy, and her innocence had touched him in a way no other before had ... and she'd *responded* to him.

She'd kissed him, her tongue mingling with his, twisting her mouth against his, and she'd asked him blearily, 'Who *are* you?'

He'd told her he was her new husband, that it was their wedding night and in her far-out state she'd nodded acceptance and received him in all his glory ... He arched his back as he spent himself with perfect timing.

Afterwards, he dwelt on Miller. *You're going to pay for that, Miller. Just as soon as I get fixed up, I'll find a way.* He cleaned himself up, and settled down to read the book.

People who shouldn't have had been talking about him. *No fuckin' loyalty.* He wondered if she'd spoken to the Flynns. She'd talked to his aunts about the bad influence his father was.

With a dad like that he never stood a chance; lying, thieving, work-shy – and he was a pervert to boot. His mother did her best to save Martin, but it was too late. He'd walked in the darkness and he liked it. While she was alive, he never strayed too far over the line, that we know of, though there was an incident with a girl when he was younger. Something happened, but it was all glossed over. Apparently, one of the Flynn girls caught him peeping in through a window at her undressing, but he had some excuse ... he was looking for his lost cat, and he'd heard it meowing ...

Looking back and seeing the excuse on paper made him realize how lame it was. Things he hadn't thought about in a long time found their way to the surface. Mary Flynn. She used to drive him crazy with those hot pants she always wore – and he'd actually loved her. They'd go off together into the woods. He'd recite passages by Hollywood actors and have her compare his voice to tapes he'd made of them, played back on an old tinny cassette player. Then they'd fuck. He loved to bite her lips. She wasn't so keen. His lips thinned, as close to a fond smile as he'd ever been. But the old man fucked things up for him because he'd had to go back to get rid of him and, afterwards, he'd had to burn the caravan down.

It was a long time before he went back. At first he'd missed Mary, but his mother always came through, reminding him, 'Mary never really liked you, anyway.'

There had been only two female loves in his life at that time. His mother and Mary.

Unnatural love, but that, again, was his father's fault.

The sound of teeth clacking together twice snapped his attention back.

Did I just do that? His father used to do that. *Oh, no, you don't!* He shook his head. *I got rid of you years ago.*

Did you, Son, did you? The apple don't fall far from the tree.

He bunched his fist and shook it at the empty air. His left forefinger had dutifully held his place in the book. *Not fuckin' true. You'd never have learned to read ... I'm nothing like you.*

From the shadows a voice, filled with loathing, breathed, '*No, you're not. You're worse.*'

As if in defiance, he leered, closed the book, sniffed its edges again, and then ran his tongue all the way around it.

The lumpy pillow folded in half, he lifted the hat from his head, placed it over his face and fell asleep with the taste of her in his mouth.

Chapter 5

Boyle is known to have kidnapped at least three women, including two sisters. One of them, Kathy ... he kept like an animal for twenty-three years before she was rescued. Her ordeal at his hands left her mentally and physically scarred. He'd cut through her top lip with scissors, and then stitched it roughly together again, so it looked like she had his mother's mouth. That's one sick individual.

Anonymous police source

Determined not to get caught in the noonday sun again, Carla rose early, showered and leisurely caressed her skin in the lukewarm water. Washing her hair, she watched the trail of lather run between her breasts and down over her abdomen, and bubble in the places it gathered below the vertical line of her tattoo. Tracing the tiny letters with her fingertip, she thought briefly about Miller, and then leaned back, savouring the coolness of the tiled surface. A moment later, she shrugged herself upright and, pirouetting slowly, rinsed herself beneath the jets before stepping out.

After dressing, she admired her look in the mirror. She wondered whether she revealed too much of her shape in her skinny jeans. A plain white cotton top chosen, she let it drape to cover part of her backside. Satisfied, she collected her bag and keys, and unplugged her phone from its charger. *Damn! Still flat.* She wiggled the lead, and then the phone chimed as power began flowing into it. Should she wait? No. She'd come back for it in a couple of hours.

Early-morning bustling sounds assailed her senses, stimulating a strange sort of excitement. Vibrant colours drew her gaze.

Discarding the ceramics, hangings and rugs, she tried focusing on other items of interest – leather goods of every size and shape abundantly displayed, piled high, as was everything else, it seemed, in an effort to draw customers' attention. And drums, every kind of drum. Finger drums and tom-toms. *How do they make a living from them when there's so much competition?* With every available nook and cranny filled with goods, stalls displaying items of clothing drew her eyes.

As she wandered towards them she caught the heady aroma of the local *kif* and the scent triggered recognition, inducing a memory high. She grinned to herself, finally becoming at ease, and sauntered, browsing in search of something different to wear, to take home with her. Tomorrow, she'd pack and take the bus to Marrakech.

It occurred to her to ask Mohammed, if she saw him in time, how much his father would want to take her. Four hours of Babylon, as she'd affectionately nicknamed him: she didn't think she could take it.

Sudden awareness led her thinking to shift; something had caught her attention and registered. Ahead, a man walked with a familiar gait, stirring subconscious memories as she stared at his back. He was heavily built, and from his yellow hair she guessed he was a German tourist. The robe he wore stopped halfway down his calves. Absently looking down at his feet, she noticed he was wearing cowboy boots, and fanning himself with a leather hat. He turned.

It's him! The shock threw her out of gear, but instinct propelled her away. Imagining he might have her fixed in his sights, she tensed and thought quickly. A few yards ahead, a stall was selling traditional garb, burqas and headscarves. She spotted a turquoise range, selected a half-niqab and tied it quickly while the stallholder fussed over her, getting it right, amazed when she didn't attempt any bartering.

Without looking back, she headed towards the top of the market while he appeared to be engrossed in jars of herbs crudely labelled as Viagra. *Jesus, even if that stuff doesn't work, if he thinks it does* ... She shuddered at the thought. Turning into a road at the outer limit of the market, away from the crowds, she sought to double back on herself around the outskirts. After passing a series of foul-smelling bins, she found herself in a dead end.

The heat behind the veil was almost unbearable and she pulled on it in a bellows action to cool her face. Tempted to remove it, she retraced her footsteps and turned back around the corner to find another way out. *Shit!*

Boyle was clomping up the street in her direction, no more than twenty feet away. With evasion impossible, she took a deep breath and coolly walked past him, staring straight ahead. Once she'd passed him, the urge to run was irresistible and she fought to contain it. *A few more paces and I'll turn into another street ... keep calm, Carla ...* She realized that in her initial haste to find her way out she'd overshot the street that would take her to safety. *Just another few paces ...*

Behind her, Boyle sniffed the air and turned. Clearly visible through the crowd, he made out her tall and slender form. *It's her!*

Unsteadily, in boots he'd not quite grown accustomed to, he quickened his pace, barging through the crowd, trying not to lose sight of her.

She turned the corner unaware that, behind her, he had broken into a run.

Immediately she was off the main thoroughfare, she ran. The street ahead was crowded with people, mostly tourists still arriving for the market. Rattling scooters and whining mopeds added to the din and muddled her thoughts. *The main road must be near.*

She slowed and glanced over her shoulder. Boyle hurtled around the corner, feet scrambling for purchase as he took it in a wide arc, narrowly avoiding collision with a group of elderly locals who'd stopped to talk. *Jesus, he's coming fast. Oh, great, now he's seen me!*

Adrenaline injected urgent pace into her limbs. She took flight. Everything zoned out from her mind; survival mode zeroed in to only what was necessary for escape, and yet she heard the slap-slap-slap of her feet and the heavy pounding of his boots. She realized, comparing the cadence, that she needed to go faster. Her thighs burned, complaining at the unexpected effort placed on them. *At the gym at least I get to warm up. Why didn't I take my shoes off?* Dodging in and out of the crowds, she chanced another look behind. He'd closed the gap between them to ten yards.

Turning her head forward again she almost collided with a tourist who'd stopped abruptly to look at his guide map. Quickly sidestepping, and then launching into a sprint, her legs jellified. *I can't keep this up.* She felt the heat of Boyle's gaze boring into her shoulder blades. Scanning the street ahead for an escape route, she realized there was nowhere to go. He would catch her in seconds. A door opened to the left. Sounds, cacophonous in her head, blended with the thump of her pounding heart. Legs gone, she attempted to divert into the inviting aperture. The high drone of an engine screamed into her consciousness. A moped screeched its brakes. She was about to be run over.

At the last moment it swerved, tyres squealing, missing her by inches.

'Quickly, lady, jump on!'

Mohammed! A last burst of strength powered her limbs, and she leaped onto the seat as the boy shot forwards. Boyle's hand raked her back, grabbing a handful of her blouse as the bike accelerated, groaning under the weight of two passengers. The momentum and the killer's grip on her clothing forced her backwards. Leaning precariously, at the point of tipping off, she grabbed Mohammed's waist, her blouse ripping from her back as they took off, weaving precariously between shocked pedestrians.

The last thing she saw as she anxiously checked behind was Boyle left holding the remnants of her blouse in his hand. Scowling at onlookers, he crumpled the blouse into a ball, and shoved it down the front of his jeans before disappearing from view.

Chapter 6

A familiar and persistent discomfort every time Boyle's right foot went down confirmed his self-diagnosis; he didn't even have to look. *She's given you a blister.* He grinned. *When I catch hold of you, I'll give you a blister you'll not forget in a hurry.*

After locating his vehicle in the packed car park, he opened the door. A scorching burst of heat blasted out. Before taking his seat, he quickly wound the windows down and then started the engine.

The queue to the exit crawled. The slow movement, generating no welcome circulation of air, did little to dissipate the sweltering heat although, as he turned, a sea breeze wafted in bringing with it a slight drop in temperature. Tempted to cut through the wrong way, he nudged the truck out to begin the manoeuvre, but noticed a policeman observing him closely. It was the one from the shop. Recognizing him, he raised a hand to Boyle who responded with a clenched fist and as broad a fake smile as he could muster. The officer approached. Suddenly the blouse tucked down the front of his jeans felt as large as a bed sheet.

'*Bonne journée. Comment êtes-vous, Monsieur pugiliste?*'

Still grinning, Boyle waved his hand in front of his face and coughed deeply, aggravating his throat into a genuine and prolonged hacking. Eyes watering, he whispered hoarsely, pointing to his throat. '*Je n'ai pas de voix ...*'

A gap opened in the queue. The officer stepped back a pace, clearly not wishing to catch his ailment, and waved him on.

Fifteen minutes. He hadn't a prayer of finding them on the streets and resolved to go back to his room.

On the way, he speculated on where she might be staying. It would be a good hotel, he decided. Possibly one with a sea view. He assessed the possibilities. *That's it. That's where she'll be. And who was that little shit on the scooter?*

Turning the vehicle round, he headed for the hotel he had in mind.

'Nearly, we are here,' Mohammed, voice barely audible above the rattling engine, called back.

He hadn't stopped babbling on and turning around to look at her since he'd assisted with her escape.

'No worry, lady, at mine house I have new clothes for you.' He paused. 'They are my mother's. But she doesn't mind if you take ...'

Fortunately, the front and sleeves of the blouse remained. However, she was acutely aware of the need to cover up at the first opportunity. Her mind raced ahead. She hadn't expected to encounter Boyle. It changed everything. He'd have come after her anyway, once he'd got so far through her book. One thing puzzled her. *He seemed to know I'd be there.* Frowning, unable to find an immediate answer, she realized Mohammed had steered through a series of narrowing streets, the engine's urgent labours sounding less frenetic, but doubled in echoing volume by the claustrophobic closeness of the high enclosing walls.

He pulled in beside a shabbily maintained white wall and directed her to a faded and flaking painted blue door, one of the many set into the walls either side of them.

'Welcome to mine house,' he said, opening the door and, with a nod of the head, indicating that she should enter.

'Mohammed, I didn't get the chance to say – I'm glad to see you – but tell me, how did you know it was me under that veil?'

He grinned vaguely and shrugged bashfully. 'You ask me to look out for you ...'

'But you were nowhere near ...'

'My friends, they follow, see what happens with the man and phone me – "Come quickly!" So I come.'

Following him in through the lobby, she realized it was an apartment and not a house. They passed a communal staircase.

Mohammed led her to a dimly lit corner behind it and unlocked the door.

Inside, a long passageway led through to the kitchen.

'Where is your mother, Mohammed?'

'I have no mother. She is died.' He shrugged and looked at the floor. 'Now, in the day, it is only me.'

'I'm sorry,' she said. Her gaze took in the sparse surroundings. The only non-essential items were pictures of his family. 'Where are your brothers and sisters?'

'They are in school.' Following her gaze to the photographs, he said, 'No look. Now come, first you tell me ... who is that man? Then we find you dress.'

'I can't tell you much. You helped me put those posters up ... I've written a book about him, and he doesn't like me.' She paused and said gently, 'I don't want to put you in any danger; your family needs you. All I need is something else to wear, and then I'll get a taxi ... your father ... do you think he could take me to the airport?'

'He is there, now, in Marrakech. When he come back, of course he take you.'

'Marrakech? When will he be back?'

'Maybe four, maybe five hours.'

'I can't wait that long. I'll find someone else.'

Disappointment crossed his face; then his eyes lit up. 'No, lady. *I* will take you. Airport is ten minutes from here.'

'Shit!' she exclaimed.

'What is ... *shit?*'

'I can leave my clothes ...' she said, 'but my passport, and phone ... I have to go back to the hotel for those.'

'Lady,' he said, sternly. 'This is job for Mohammed.'

'I know you'd like to help, but I can't let you do that.'

'You have key to hotel room?'

'You're not going.'

'Wait, one moment.' He disappeared from the room. On his return, he carried an assortment of robes and sandals. 'This for you. Mother was slim, not high like you, but it is better than you have ...' Casting his eyes over her torn blouse, he jerked his head at her. 'And your jeans,' he said, tongue playing across his lips. 'You must take off, or too much hot with this *djebella*.' He offered it to her from the top of the pile.

Does he really think ... She shook her head slowly, examining his gawky frame and then said with humour, 'Nice try … How old are you?'

'No matter ...' He grinned and straightened himself with pride. 'I am a man.'

Lifting the plain blue hooded garment, she resisted the urge to crinkle her nose at the staleness of it. 'I have a feeling this might come in useful.'

'This from when Mother is a young woman, we never throw. When Jamilla is big, she will wear.' He looked at her feet. 'And this ... Take these.' He shoved a pair of sandals at her.

She removed her footwear. The boy tutted at her painted nails. 'This feet, are no good. I have the sock for this. You wear sock.'

'Not on your life. I know Englishmen have a reputation for wearing socks with sandals, but no way, you're kidding me.'

'No way,' he echoed, not fully understanding. 'OK, now give key.'

'Mohammed ...' she drawled.

'In ten minutes, I am there. In ten minutes, I am back. What is problem?' he snorted. 'Him, he does not know me. Give me key, and I am back before you finish dress up in Mother's clothes.'

She hesitated, weighing the options, and then placed the key in his hand. 'Be careful,' she said, and ruffled his hair. 'I'll see you in a few minutes.'

Mohammed sat astride his scooter and punched a series of numbers into his telephone. Engaged. He cursed and started the scooter, keeping the revs down until he cleared the end of his street.

Outside the hotel he again dialled a number, this time connecting. He babbled in a melange of Arabic and French before disconnecting and going to the rear entrance.

A porter appeared, opening the doorway. 'Quickly,' he hissed. 'No one must see you.'

Mohammed followed him in.

'Which room is it?'

He showed him the key. 'Upstairs, top floor. I trust you, do not be seen.' He exhaled. 'Get her things, then you go.' They touched fists.

He took the steps two at a time; the only sounds came from the cleaners in the rooms. At the top, he peered cautiously along the corridor, not unduly worried. He shouldn't be there, but he knew almost everyone and he was sure if he were accosted he would talk his way out of trouble.

A single cleaner's trolley occupied a space outside one of the rooms. His heart sank. *This is her room.* He produced the key as evidence he had a right to be there, inhaled deeply and stepped through the open door into the room.

For a moment he assumed the cleaner was elsewhere. He stole along the passageway, imagining he might get in and out again without the need for an explanation.

The room was cool. *Ah, the perfume of the cleaner.* No sound, but he smelt her. Stirring senses alerted him to an odd smell mingled with her fragrance.

Stale sweat. Sometimes the cleaners should clean themselves. Fatima, it can only be, but she is quiet.

The bathroom door opened noiselessly behind him as he crept further into the bedroom. *Nobody is here. Good.* The telephone was plainly visible on the bedside cabinet. A large valise was tucked in a corner. *The passport. She say it is on cabinet; maybe she put it in the draw?* Paper ruffled underfoot; he looked down.

The image staring back at him from the poster was the man from the market. When they were pasting them up everywhere he hadn't looked real, but having seen him in the flesh … He shuddered as he stepped clear and immediately pitched forwards and down, driven by the force of a mighty hand pushing his head towards the floor. Fingers dug in hard, seeking purchase around his neck.

Mohammed dipped low and twisted around. Seeing the cleaner sprawled lifeless on the floor in the bathroom, his eye shot a reflex glance between her legs, at her exposed pubic hair. The first part of the man he saw was his scuffed cowboy boots.

With the boy securely pinned to the floor, Boyle took the room key from his hand. 'Billy bloody whizz,' he said, recognizing him. 'Where is she?'

Still held down, unable to move, Mohammed thought quickly. *I cannot die.* He would find a way to escape. 'I show you,' he said, quaking with fear.

Boyle spun him over, staring into his face intently while his free hand found its way around the boy's testicles. 'You tell me now,' he growled quietly. 'Or you'll never see another day.'

Chapter 7

With Mohammed gone and his father not due home for hours, Carla changed into her new garb. The kid was right. She'd be too hot keeping her jeans on. She removed them and, rolling them up, put them in her bag ready to take with her. Dressed in his mother's clothes, she awaited his return. It felt strange. More than once, unusually for her, she found herself worrying. She couldn't help but empathize with him, and his life. Looking around the apartment, she imagined it filled with his siblings, mother fussing around, father never there, and Mohammed taking on the role in his absence.

She crossed the room to the photographs and lingered, examining them more closely. Now she understood why he'd said 'no look'. His mother was dressed in what she was now wearing. The fond smile on her lips disappeared. She frowned. The stale odour of the clothes was getting to her. The tang held far more than mere smell and she knew it, yet couldn't define it. She imagined briefly what it must have been like to be the matriarch in that household. And then a thought settled on her.

Something's wrong. She felt it as surely as if she were there with him. *He's in trouble.* What had she been thinking, allowing the boy to go off like that? Her reluctance to involve the police – because the story was in Boyle coming after her, coming to England – had led her into placing the boy in danger. The way she'd planned it suddenly seemed inconsequential. For a moment she dithered, then – mind made up – she grabbed her bag, removed an atomizer, sprayed puffs of cologne over herself to mask the mustiness of the clothes, and resolved to go and find him.

Making her way from the rabbit warren of streets and alleyways took longer than she'd thought. After flagging down a taxi driver on the main road, she soon arrived at her hotel.

Ambulances and police cars, with lights flashing, ringed the entrance. A crowd had gathered in the car park.

'What's happened?' she asked a bystander, anxiously.

'Someone's been murdered, and ...'

A huge wave of guilt rose inside her, shutting her off from everything. Walking like an automaton, she slipped through the melee in the foyer unnoticed, as if she were a ghost. She reached the desk and asked for her key. The receptionist told her she couldn't go to her room.

'My passport,' she said. 'I need my passport ...'

From the corner of her eye, she noticed barely perceptible glances exchanged. The porter moved slowly away, towards a policeman.

He spoke to the officer, who brushed him away.

The boy persisted, pointing at her. The officer looked up. Their eyes met.

Her mind switched from the depths of agonized guilt to her own predicament. All logic left her. She made an instant decision, and one she probably shouldn't have.

She ran.

Chapter 8

Heart pounding in her ears, her breath became ragged as she fought to control it. Zig-zagging through the bustling crowd, she cleared the car park, turned left and ran towards the market. At home she could run for miles, but this was different. Adrenaline surging through her veins made pacing herself difficult. Uncertain of how much longer she could run, she threw a glance over her shoulder. Sure enough, less than fifty yards away, two gendarmes were chasing her.

She paused at an intersecting alleyway. Left or right?

An arm snaked out, wrapping itself around her waist from behind, and jerked her into a doorway.

Instinctively clawing at the jambs, she dug her fingernails in.

Time slowed down. She sucked in air to scream. A hand clamped tight over her mouth, muffling the sound. Her bladder puckered. She kicked out with both legs, dropping her weight, digging her heels hard against the pavement. Bending her legs for additional purchase, she drove backwards with a force that surprised her. Locked together, their two bodies tumbled off balance and crashed down hard. She landed on top of her assailant.

'No – scream – lady!' he hissed, wincing with pain.

'Mohammed? But I thought ...?' She paused to regain her composure. 'They said ... somebody said there'd been a murder, and I thought ...'

'Yes, him try murder me, too.'

'You saw him?'

'Lady, he in your room. He squeeze mine balls, and say, "Tell where is she." And I fight, lady, very hard for you, but my balls ...'

'Did you tell him where I was?' she asked gently.

He looked down. 'Yes. I think maybe I get away, tell you, go! But he take me on balcony and throw me off ...'

'But how did you survive ... you don't seem hurt.'

'My balls is hurt,' he protested. 'But I catch wall, next one down.' He lifted his T-shirt revealing ugly bruising and scraped, raw flesh. 'I run here, and I am fainted, I think.' He grimaced.

'You must go to hospital, Mohammed. Are you hurt anywhere else?'

He shook his head.

'You may have broken some ribs ...'

'Leave me, I be OK,' he said.

Hesitant, she chewed on her lower lip. 'Did you get my passport?'

'No, he take ... Oh, lady, I am scared. You must go to police. This man very bad.'

She knew what he said was true. Her mind raced through the possibilities. 'Mohammed, I need you to trust me. When I go, he will follow, and he will never come back. When I get my story ...'

The boy shook his head and said with quiet certainty. 'He will kill you, and your story ... it is nothing for you then.'

She considered her answer. 'It's for the children I don't yet have.' *Are you lying, Carla?* Her words surprised her. She shook them from her head. 'I will return. I'll give you money for your family. I hate to ask ... But what about my phone?'

'I had in my one hand when he throw me ...' Disappointment marred his face. 'I drop it.'

'Don't worry. Look, I've got to go and you're going to get yourself to the hospital.'

Barely able to contain himself, he raged inwardly – a series of suppressed grunts and mews railing behind tight-bitten lips. The coppery taste of blood sobered him. He wiped his mouth on the back of his hand, staring at its foamy redness.

Fuckin' bitch. I didn't ask for this! Fuckin' none of it. Merde! His fists, clenched and hovering, wobbled in the air as he fought back the urge to go wild.

Breathing slow and deep, he calmed himself and then, lifting her book, turned to the back and examined her face more closely.

With her image inches from his nose, he turned it through different angles, as if it were three-dimensional and he could see around her picture. Becoming aroused, he sniffed the remnants of her blouse and then, tearing it in two, propped the book up next to him.

He unzipped, unleashing himself, teasing it with the soft fabric that, not so long ago, had been against her skin. Taking the book, he introduced her photograph to his cock.

'Suck it,' he commanded.

He laid back, wrapping one half of her blouse around his cock and holding the other under his nose. Imagination took him over; masturbating furiously, he cried out at the moment of ejaculation.

'I'll fuckin' ruin your cunt,' he growled, and then – staring closely at her monochrome, captive face – ran a trail of sperm across her lips. 'That's right, you like that, don't you? You goin' to fuckin' love it.'

He scissored his fingers, and snipped at her lips.

He would find her, and he'd keep her.

'Gonna fuckin' ruin ya,' he whispered.

Snuggling into a more comfortable position, he slept.

He dreamed about Kathy. A huge, aching ball of longing lodged in the pit of his stomach.

Voices. Chiding him. Mocking him. His mother and his father. He tried to shut them out, closing the door on them. His father's parting shot stabbed him. *You know someone else is fucking her now!* Although the thought angered him, it turned him on in a strange way, too.

At first light, he didn't immediately climb out of bed; reaching for the book instead, he leafed through to where he'd read up to previously, thinking there might be some news on Kathy.

The next few pages were not absorbed. His mother was back, telling him he wasn't capable of feeling, that he had no feelings, that his idea of love was obsession. A compulsive desire to possess ... *Same as your father.* The words stung him.

'I'm not anything like him!' he roared.

The apple—

'Shut up! Can't you see I'm reading?' He looked around the room. Nobody there. Silence. His thoughts stilled, he read on.

He'd only heard her voice once, but it was with him as his lips moved silently, and his finger traced the lines following her narration.

'I have the confession to make; I am with cancer. I never believe in God before, but now? I want to believe … I want to believe I can be forgiven. But for you, only confession in small part. The priest, he will have the rest.'

Henri! Boyle mused on God. *What is it that people fear? Their gods don't scare me.* His eidetic memory triggered, he remembered every time he'd ever said or even thought that. The kid with the seashell god. The Congolese priest and his god. The girl on the ferry: *Oh, my God!* And more, many more. Not one thing bad had happened to him. If he was so bad, and there was a God, he'd have struck him down.

Henri was speaking again, his voice crystal clear in Boyle's head.

'He took to the Legion like it was made for him. No one asked questions. He kept himself to himself, slowly gaining respect. I don't think I've ever known someone learn to speak French so quickly. He had this incredible memory ... I knew what he was and in the camouflage of war and turbulence, no one else noticed. So he raped and killed women in Chad, the Congo and other places. Let me explain. Before I knew this, he saved my life one day ...'

Boyle drifted back in time. He'd hung back from the others hoping to find a woman. He'd heard voices rising in anger behind one of the few mud huts that remained intact. Instinct told him to flee, but curiosity demanded he look. Henri was stripped naked, beaten, and on his knees. The mob's leader had a cleaver raised, his crazed eyes focused on the back of his stricken comrade's neck.

Boyle shot him without hesitation. The bullet struck him high on the shoulder, spinning him around. Their eyes met momentarily. He strode purposefully towards the mob who, in unison, were also turning towards *him*, some half-falling and scrambling in their eagerness to attack him. Their faces were masks of hatred.

He shot cleaver-man in the face and marched, shooting, right into the fray, emptying his gun, using it as a club at close range – bobbing, weaving, coshing with it.

When he'd finished, all that remained of a dozen men lay dead or unconscious on the ground.

A warrior appeared from around the corner with a spear drawn back, launching it with all his might. He remembered how he'd surprised even himself when he caught it. The look on the other man's face was a picture. He grinned as he remembered how he'd run him through with it, and behind the thrower ... the women and large-eyed children cowering at his feet. He'd felt like a god, the power of life or death in his hands – and in that moment he had ejaculated. He remembered it well, knowing if he had not he might have left Henri for a little while ...

His eyes refocused on the page.

'We ... It was the spoils of war for us. I joined him. He'd never had a friend before. And I had the fascination, you understand? He was crazy, but smart. At first, the other men thought he was, how you say – poof. Never joined us whoring. Always he went somewhere else, alone. One night, I followed him. I should have intervened, but I was drunk, crazy with hash ... and *je ne sai quoi* ... maybe I don't live tomorrow ...'

He skipped over the rest of the lines, pausing to read where Carla had noted that he was extremely well endowed with a penis, when erect, some nine or ten inches long. She speculated this might have been one reason he found it difficult to maintain a relationship.

Stupid bitch. Maintain a fuckin' relationship? Kath loved it! 'You'll find out for yourself in a little while,' he breathed, and flicked over the page.

'I didn't see him again until 1981. Then two, maybe three years later, he visited with his wife to meet me for a holiday, you know? Very quiet woman, with beautiful eyes. She have the harelip like him, follow him like a puppy, but you know ... something in the eyes, she is not happy.'

What's this the bitch is saying?

'Following the interview with my source, I searched the archives to see if any disappearances had coincided with his trips to France and nothing showed up that could be linked to him. However, I did come across a report of a young girl who'd disappeared on her way back from France while on a ferry. After more research, I discovered something very interesting. William Boyle had used his Foreign Legion name, Boule, to board the boat, the same one the girl had disappeared from ...' *Clever bitch.* He shook his head in grudging admiration. Oh, how he was going to enjoy his revenge.

He took a perverse delight in reading about himself; her unbiased style of reporting had him thinking they'd get on well together, the same as Kathy, once she got to know him better. As for Henri, he was glad that cancer had got him. Saved him a job. *Might have to put him outta his misery. That's what friends are for.* A moment of fleeting regret, an acknowledgement of the disappearance of youthful things, touched him. He was more tired than he'd been in ages. *It was that little bitch with the bat started it off when she clobbered you.* He still had the old march-or-die mentality in him, but for how long?

Got business to do ... Yet, his thoughts meandered on.

He remembered how he'd gone out on the boat deck ... he felt his cock stiffen. *Jesus, this thing ...* It was one thing his dad was right about. *You can't let your cock rule your head – it's got no brains.*

Flipping the book over, he stared at her photo, coolly assessing her. *You ain't going anywhere without your passport. Oh, and the way you snoop, you know about that body in your room, and the kid, by now. You can't afford to go to the police. No, and if I had to guess your next move, it'd be what you think I would think that you wouldn't do. You're going to go overland.* His fingers traced her mouth. *No time for that now. You're still here, and I've got to get out there and find you.*

Chapter 9

Miller hated flying. It hadn't helped that the passenger next to him, a young Spanish woman, had been silently counting off the beads of her rosary ever since take off. She appeared to have put herself into a transcendental state. Apart from the movement of her fingers over the religious talisman, she'd hardly moved during the flight. Now, as the aeroplane began its descent, she crossed herself three times, and returned to whispering her inaudible prayers.

'Say one for me,' he said.

She regarded him with irritation, and returned to the previous bead.

'OK,' he said, grinning. 'I'll say one for both of us.'

He braced himself hard, legs rigid, pushing himself back into his seat as the aircraft touched down, tyres squealing in protest as it bounced, engines in reverse, roaring. He noted from the corner of his eye that she had mimicked his position, hips slightly raised from the seat, their legs strangely parallel. The aeroplane decelerated rapidly, slowing and taxiing into position. They relaxed in unison, relieved at landing safely. The rest of the passengers on the aeroplane clearly shared the sentiment; the deck filled with the massed sound of unmistakably excited voices chattering in a multitude of different languages, punctuated by the metallic unclipping of seatbelts.

He turned to the raven-haired girl and smiled. 'Thanks for getting us down safely.'

She flashed small white teeth, and tossed her corkscrew hair to one side. 'It works for me every time.'

She was about the same age as Stella. A sense of guilt unexpectedly washed over him; she had so much wanted to join him, and he had done something he hadn't wanted to. He'd gone back on his word, deciding that the trip was too dangerous. 'Look, Stella,' he'd said. 'It's going to be bad enough looking out for one other person apart from me. Two people ... It's best if you stay. If something went wrong and you fell into his hands ...'

'You don't even know that he's there ...' she said.

'He is,' he replied with certainty, a hand on each of her shoulders, holding her at arm's length. The expression on his face left her in no doubt that he believed himself to be right.

'How do you see these things?' she said. 'I mean, you've told me some of it before, but you always hold back, never tell me *exactly* how.'

'It's because I don't know all of it. She put something in me when I left you with Ryan that last time.'

'You mean the Sister?'

'Yes. I was seeing more and more before we met. It's to do with our original link-up, but now she turns me on and off like a surveillance camera ...'

'But why would she do that?'

His brow furrowed. 'I have no idea.'

With Stella's help, he had successfully narrowed down the search for Carla, using Google search images. The blue doors, the castle walls and the seagulls clinched it for him. *Mogador.* Now known as Essaouira.

Exiting the terminal, he ignored the attentions of the many would-be porters and got into a taxi. His valise placed on the floor between his legs, he instructed the driver. 'Take me to the best hotel in Essaouira.'

Despite her insistence, Mohammed would not go to the hospital.

'If I go, what happen to you? What you do, lady, you stay here? Mohammed, he say, no, you go.' His brown eyes settled on her face; he wouldn't meet her gaze.

She stared at him; amazed at his loyalty to someone he didn't really know. 'I have to go,' she said simply.

'Then I take you. Where you go – aeroport?'

She thought ahead. She needed to lose Mohammed. She couldn't allow him to place himself in jeopardy; it was imperative she stayed put. *How am I going to work this out?*

'Lady—'

'Shush, Mohammed, I'm thinking,' she said. The boy placed his hands together and gazed skywards in mock prayer.

Boyle would think she'd run. He would know she couldn't go to the police. *Maybe I'll have to.* She was in two minds for only a few moments. *Can't risk the airport.* Boyle would go to the docks, thinking she'd try for a boat. Weighing possibility against chance, her face lit up with inspiration. *Overland!*

She'd wait until morning and go cross-country, while he was busy watching the harbour. Where could she stay meanwhile? With no passport, a hotel was out of the question. *Mohammed.*

'Where is your bike?'

'In car park. Why – you want me take you somewhere?'

She bit her lip. 'Do you think your father would mind if I—'

'Lady, when he is not here, I am the father. You wanted stay at mine house?'

She lowered her eyes demurely. 'Yes.'

'I go then, for bike,' he beamed. 'Wait here, I come back.'

A slab of light cast itself across the tiled floor as he opened the door, disappearing as he shut it behind him. Her eyes, dazzled by the sudden glare, gradually readjusted, and she took in her surroundings for the first time. Light penetrated the small windows at high level. It appeared he'd pulled her into the lobby of a disused building.

She started to think about Boyle and wondered if he'd actually picked up a copy of her book, and if he *had* – if he'd got to the passage where she'd summarized everything she'd learned to date. That part had followed her visit to one of his former neighbours. A previous interviewer, acting under the guise of researching material for a book on the greatest bare-knuckle fighters of the twentieth century, had almost blown it for her with his insensitive handling of the Gypsy elder.

She recalled the initial meeting she had with him.

'Who did you say sent you again?' Archie Brooks eyed her with suspicion.

She smiled, dipping her head so that she looked at him from beneath the spiky fringe of her black hair. 'Didn't I tell you on the phone? Nobody *sent* me; I was passed your details by a fellow writer, Mr Quinn. I believe you met—'

'Him!' he spat. 'Something I didn't like about that boy, asked too many questions he did.' He paused, light glinting in the stony chippings his narrowed eyes had become. 'He's not your man, is he?'

'Good Lord, no! Is it all right if I call you Archie?' She extended her hand, adding: 'I'd have to be dead to be lying with him.'

Brooks grinned. 'Come in, Clara,' he said.

'Carla,' she corrected, and stepped inside.

She hoped that he'd forgive her for misquoting him, justifying it, just as she had when she first wrote the piece. *It's for the greater good and not only for the people, but my purse too.* Taking the voice recorder from her bag, she dictated an update to her story so far.

It was the sound that drew her back from recording the notes or, more correctly, an explosion, followed by a dread moment of silence. Followed by screams. She floated as if disconnected from reality as her body lurched towards the door, and opened it. The harsh glare of sunshine stung her eyes, and she was torn in two.

Lying mangled in the road, a white and chrome scooter pop-popped, engine dying, headlight pointing upwards at a crazy angle – and underneath, crushed, rag doll-like and staring with sightless eyes ... *Mohammed.*

Women wailed. A lanky tourist, in a desert outfit of military-like khaki, attended on the boy, and then stepped away, shaking his head. A woman covered her face, and began ululating. Other women joined in. Realizing nothing could be gained by her continuing presence, Carla took flight.

Chapter 10

Pain. Not his. Someone else's. Miller gazed out through the passenger window thinking the source lay beyond, in the streets.

A dark shape lurched across his field of vision. Bracing himself, he jammed his foot down on imaginary brakes.

The driver reacted to his passenger's physical cue, his foot leaving the accelerator, touching the brake pedal. The taxi's speed dropped. He scanned the road ahead for what had caused the reflex action of the man next to him. *Nothing.*

'What for you do that?' the driver said.

Miller closed his eyes and applied pressure to the length of his nose with his forefinger, the tip curling across its bridge to a point between his eyes. The relief was instant.

'Oh, that ... it was nothing. I do that sometimes. I have this pain. It makes me do that.'

The other man nodded. 'Sometimes, after many hours' drive. Mine head with pain.' Two fingers forked as he indicated his eyes. 'Too much look. You understand?'

Miller stared out of the window. 'Yes, too much look. I understand.'

'English, no? If I practise the English ... speak with you, you don't mind?' Without waiting for agreement, he pressed on.

Miller switched off. Something had happened, somewhere. He knew it. He felt it. He just couldn't see it. *Yet.* And that was something else he knew. He *would* see. Turning over the impressions forming in his mind, he tuned in to them, unable to get beyond a barrage of static interference. The driver interrupted his thoughts.

'You like music? Here very big festival in June, you miss. Ten, twenty thousand people, they come. That place, you see?' Leaning over, he pointed up the street. 'In there, you cannot see from here. Always there is music. Always. Today is very special man play guitar. Him, Spanish. With him, blind man. He play the ...' Lost for words, he blew out his cheeks, one hand at his breast, the other at his abdomen, waggling his fingers on invisible keys.

'The saxophone?' Miller ventured.

'Saxophone,' the driver repeated slowly. 'Yes, that is him.'

The car turned right into the next street. A crowd blocked the road. All heads were facing in the same direction. Nobody moved.

The blind man ... You see ...

Miller zeroed in on the scene and triangulated points that had previously made no sense. *A broken boy, seen from above.*

Magnetism, manifested and mingled, mixing with the man next to him. He felt what the driver wouldn't feel for a few moments yet.

Pain. A knot formed in his belly. At last, he understood. He'd had a premonition. It was linked to the man next to him. The warning had come too late, and there wasn't a thing he could do about it.

'I'll get out here,' Miller said, erasing the image of carnage from his mind's eye. The taxi crawled to a halt. 'Thank you,' he said, overpaying the fare. The driver's jubilant thanks fell on deaf ears as he strode down to the next street. From there, he'd make his way to the music bar. He didn't need to walk past the accident scene. He'd already seen it.

Carla pulled the niqab about her face and forced herself to walk, her head a busy terminal of thoughts landing and taking off again. There was a danger of losing it, she knew that. The what-ifs and self-recrimination built up uncontrollably, blocking her escape. Possibilities needed to land. What would happen to Mohammed's family? How would they cope? It was her fault. All of it. Nothing she could ever do would make it right. And here she was in his mother's clothes, unfit to wear them.

Not given to God-fearing, she surprised herself by making up the words to a prayer and mouthing it, imploring God, whoever He may be, to smile on Mohammed, and look after him. He was but a child after all. She conjured a vision of him standing in a radiant white light. His mother emerged from its brilliance, serene, welcoming, holding out her hand. He took it. They turned and walked away, the light clothing them. Her teeth hurt. Tears smarted her eyes. She sniffed once and wiped them dry. She hurried away in the direction of the hotel, convinced Boyle – if it was him – would have been going the other way.

A single saxophone parp caught her attention. A crowd had gathered. A bluesman had elevated himself from the ground, standing on something she couldn't see. He tilted his head back, jet-black glasses reflecting the sun, and raising his instrument, fingers flying, he blasted out an Ali Baba snake-charmer's tune. The mass of people roared its approval. Momentarily losing her bearings, and unsure which way to go, she turned from the throng in time to see people parting in waves, barrelled aside from behind by an as yet unseen force. A few feet in front, the crowd parted. A huge woman in a full black burqa bore down on her. Through still with misty eyes, she looked down below the hemline. *Cowboy boots? Jesus!*

Spinning on her heels, she dashed into the crowd heading for the keyhole doorway behind the sax man.

Chapter 11

Despite the crowd, Miller found some elbow room at the bar and waited his turn. In the far corner a space had been cleared, and a guitarist plucked the strings gently, his ear close as he tuned the instrument.

Miller returned his attention to buying a drink. In the mirror behind the barman, he thought he saw Carla's reflection race by. Turning, he saw her unmistakable spiky black hair bobbing as she pushed her way towards the rear exit. In an instant, he went after her. His superior weight gave him an advantage and he caught up with her, steering her into the male toilets, pushing her into a cubicle. 'Shhh!' he whispered. The whites of her large blue eyes were wider than he'd ever seen them.

'I thought you were—'

He put a finger to his lips.

At the door, a burly bouncer stepped from his stool to prevent a woman entering. Boyle threw off his headgear and glared at the stunned doorman, who – confused by the second Westerner to approach wearing Muslim garb, only to discard it on entry – shook his head in disbelief as the man entered the bar behind him.

Boyle's vision quickly adjusted to the gloom. He scanned the crowds. A man in a black Stetson was tuning his guitar. Next to him, smoke curled thickly from a hashish cigarette on the edge of an ashtray, twisting upwards in the dim light. *Not here.* He spotted the exit door and brushed through the crowd. He pushed it. *Locked.*

Grinning, he pushed the ladies' toilet door open. *No one here.* Returning to the exit door, he rechecked it, pushing harder; it opened. He charged outside and, seeing no sign of her, headed for the docks.

'He's gone,' Miller said.

Her knees buckled; he caught her as she staggered.

'Should've c-come before,' she slurred, her voice drunk with emotion, and fell against him, blurting out the whole sorry story.

He stood with his arms around her, steadying her. 'Let's get out of here before anyone else comes in.'

She wiped her nose and mouth on the back of her hand and stopped by the washbasin. 'I must rinse my face,' she said.

'Nothing to dry it on.' He jerked a thumb at the filthy roller towel. 'Unless you want to use that.'

'You should have been here ...' she said, accusingly.

'Carla, it wouldn't have made any difference.' He remembered the rope analogy passed on to him by the Sister. 'Maybe the strand of his life was destined to be short. Don't worry, we're going to get you out of here.'

'Don't worry ...? You have no idea.' She slapped at his face.

He caught her hand.

Snatching it away from him, she said, 'That's it. I'm not talking about it any more. I'll deal with it in my own sweet way.' She turned on her heels, opened the door, and crossed the lobby to the ladies' toilets.

He followed as she disappeared inside, opened the door a crack and called through. 'We'll stay here until it gets dark. I'll be at the bar.'

She didn't answer.

The press of the crowd was too much. A potman, eyes half-closed, collected glasses. Miller caught his attention, gesturing with a rolled-up note that he should get them drinks. The man came over.

'One beer, one gin and tonic, *s'il vous plait*,' Miller said, pushing the note into the outstretched hand before him.

Two people vacated a table, and he wasted no time sliding into one of the empty chairs, dragging another in close with his foot.

The guitarist was three tables down. Smoke curled from the joint in his mouth, one eye squinting against it as he fine-tuned each string. He seemed to take forever. Close-up he looked older than he did from a distance. His hair, blacker than the cowboy hat he wore, seemed at odds with the lines on his face. With thin lips and hooked nose he looked cruel, yet flaming passion glowered in his hawkish eyes, awaiting release. He adjusted the microphone, directed it at the soundboard of his flamenco guitar, and switched it on. It picked up the background noise and fed it back into the room, creating the illusion that the crowd had doubled in size. Excitement rose in the voices of the tourist spectators. The locals showed little interest as the sax man walked behind the gorilla from the door, one hand on his shoulder as the big man cleared a path for him to join the waiting guitarist.

Carla appeared at the table. 'I thought you'd be by the bar,' she said, raising her voice.

'I was, but you've been ages ...'

She'd scrubbed every inch of her face clean of make-up. The strain of her recent ordeals had left her looking drawn, anguish evident in her expression, her sparkle lost.

They stared at each other without a further word. She picked up her drink, took a sip, and then downed it.

Miller raised an eyebrow.

She leaned across the table and hissed, 'How dare you raise an eyebrow at me after all I've been through.'

'Would you like another?' he said, calmly. 'By the way ... the natural look. You should do it more often. You're a corker.'

A glimmer of life returned to her face. 'I am? I don't feel it, and yes, I do want another. And another after that.'

The two musicians had taken up their respective positions. In the gloom, chinks of light cut through the gaps in the shutters, alive with minuscule particles of dust and twisting hashish cigarette smoke. It was clear there would be no singing. From his seated position, the Spaniard leaned down to the microphone and introduced himself, and then the saxophonist, in French. He was met with a ripple of applause.

Miller caught the potman's attention and, with another rolled-up note, he pointed at each of their drinks. He nodded, and continued to fill his arms and hands with bottles and glasses.

A simple strumming was how it began. A rhythm building background. With fingers delicately plucking out single melodic notes, eyes closed, and the other hand feeling for frets, he had no need of seeing; the tune unfolded from his mind, transferring to the instrument as if it were part of his body.

All eyes were on him, except those of the sax man who stood swaying, knees bent, twisting in the opposite direction to the swing of his upper body. Holding his golden instrument in both hands he moved it up, down, left and right like a ceremonial weapon, the beat driving faster and faster as the musical train rolled out free and onto the tracks. The guitarist's head bobbed in metronomic time, and he introduced a slap against the soundboard, and then another, punctuating and further driving the speed at which he played.

A curtain parted behind him and out stepped a Spanish dancer in full flamenco dress. The audience went wild.

Clothed in a red and black polka-dot dress – face pale, eyes flashing, ruby-red lips curled – she twirled and stamped, raised her arms high, one at a time, alternating between head and hip as she advanced on the guitarist. Miller was transfixed.

'Don't you think we should go somewhere quieter?' Carla shouted. Unable to make him hear, she moved her chair further round to sit right next to him. 'We need to talk,' she said directly into his ear.

'I'm enjoying this, Carla,' he said.

She queried his words with her eyebrows and, turning her head, pointed to her ear.

He leaned further towards her. 'I said, I'm enjoying this.'

She pulled his head in close so that each had their mouths at the other's ear. 'Don't watch her, talk to me,' she said, breathily. Her warm breath sent tingles through him, and he detached himself. The cries of seagulls penetrated his consciousness from outside. He was looking down at the docks.

'We're safe here for a while,' he said.

'This is totally bizarre,' she replied, perplexed.

The sax man blew a low, snake-charmer's tune. The lid rose from a giant basket, and a scantily dressed exotic dancer emerged. Hands steepled above her head, she shook her body vigorously; the short diamantè chain adorning her belly button circled like a miniature propeller. An eastern twang crept into the guitarist's repertoire. The blind man blew for all he was worth and a duel ensued, dancer to dancer, player to player, as the quartet reached a crescendo of music and movement. Someone in the crowd joined in on their souvenir bongos, and when the sound could get no higher, it abruptly ceased.

Along with the rest of the crowd, Miller applauded rapturously.

'Are you stoned?' Carla asked, accusingly.

'You don't *know* how high I've just been,' he said, 'but don't worry, I'm OK.'

Their drinks arrived. It had been a mistake allowing her to drink two so quickly in succession. The heady aroma of hashish filled the air and seemed to have an effect on her.

Determined not to dwell on Mohammed's fate, she ventured, 'You never talk about *you*, do you? Or your parents ...'

His eyes took on a faraway look. 'They belong to a separate part of me, a part I keep for my family ... My mother was horrified when everyone started calling me Miller, so I keep him and those thoughts segregated.'

She nodded as if she understood. He seemed so wise. Then she crumpled. 'Oh, Miller, make this pain go away. Or, at least, help me take my mind off it.'

'You know, Carla, pain ... it never really goes away. You can leave it behind, but it's always there, lurking in the background.'

'Get me away from here. Take me somewhere ... let's go.' She wrapped her fingers around his and leaned her head on his shoulder. 'Just a few minutes, make me forget ...'

'Carla, no. I'm with Stella now and, besides, if I have sex, I lose the edge. It's hard to explain. I lose some degree of awareness, and I think we're going to need me to have that.'

Her feelings already in turmoil, she looked hurt. 'I don't understand. You always push me away.' She paused, thoughtfully, and then shrugged. 'Anyway, why are you not telling me to go to the police? You could vouch for me, couldn't you?'

'Yes, I could, but I don't want to do that. Ever since I left home, there's been only one thing on my mind.'

Her face brightened and she pouted. 'You couldn't wait to see me again?'

'No. I'm going to find a way to kill him.'

'So that's why you're here?' She shook her head slowly. 'I should have known. Oh, and by the way ...' She thought about what she was going to say for a moment. 'Don't you think that's incredibly stupid and selfish? If you do that,' she said testily, 'you'll ruin my story.'

'Always the story ...' he said, beckoning her forward. 'If I do it right ... it'll become part of the story.'

'But how?'

He touched his nose.

'You know I hate it when you do that.'

'I know. Listen, if I'd come on my own, I wouldn't be scared of him. We'd have had our showdown. He's older now and he's had that blow to the head. He doesn't feel invincible anymore. I can beat him.'

'Then why don't you, if you're so sure ...'

'That's the trouble, because if it goes wrong – he's got you.'

'So you're not so sure?'

'It just complicates things, that's all.'

'What kind of an answer do you call that?'

'Wait here. I'll be back soon.'

On his way out, he had a word with the doorman. Pressing a few notes into his hand, he described Boyle with gestures, flattening his nose, mimicking the shape of his mouth and, when he indicated with a snip that the top of his ear was missing, the bouncer's eyes gleamed recognition. 'I know this man,' he grunted.

'Good ... Look, he's been harassing that lady.' He pointed out Carla.

She saw him and waved, looking confused.

'If this man comes, keep him out. And keep an eye on her,' he said, showing him a couple of banknotes. 'When I come back, these are for you.'

The big man stood erect, suddenly more alert. He gave Miller a curt nod.

As he left the club, he walked towards the car hire centre he'd noticed on the way in. The thought of driving suited him. The train was out of the question. Too restrictive. A car would be better for getting her overland to the ferry at Tangier. He'd make arrangements with the hire company for taking the car on a day trip, so he'd have the necessary paperwork.

The thought of having her in the boot appealed to him.

Chapter 12

The poster stuck out like a sore thumb. Miller stopped for a closer look. It was pasted onto the side wall of a clay-coloured building that fronted the square.

Emblazoned and superimposed across the top of an artist's impression, the legend read: *The Life and Times of William Boule.*

She must have had the image done since she'd sent him the book originally; she'd not only changed the cover, she'd changed the title as well. The edges of the flyer were peeling away. The middle section bulged where the glue had lost adhesion to the uneven rendered surface.

'Where are you?' he said to the image. 'What are you doing here?' For a moment he considered his own question and then looked about him at the predominantly white buildings with blue doors, at the mix of people, and got at least part of the answer: he could blend in.

Miller sensed Boyle had been here before.

A breeze rose out of nowhere; raising dust and minor detritus, it tugged at the loose paper edges, rushing below the picture. The image billowed out, as full as a sail in high wind and, unable to resist the sudden pressure, detached from the stucco, flapping for a moment from a corner that held on defiantly, until finally tearing free. Seized by warm currents of air, it was borne along and over the heads of the afternoon crowd, fluttering wildly, rising up and up like a magic carpet, before disappearing out of sight.

Staring in the direction it had taken, he shrugged his shoulders and thought, why not? If he could find him without Carla around, it would be so much better. He started after it on a hunch, in the opposite direction to the car hire centre.

After strolling for only a few minutes, Miller located a shop with *The Life and Times of William Boule* for sale. He purchased the book and a large red marker pen. Flicking through the book, he found the page he was looking for.

Twenty minutes later, having found five more posters, he walked back to hire a car.

Despite his disguise, with heightened police activity Boyle guessed it was only a question of time before he was stopped. He'd abandoned his truck and all the walking had blistered his feet. He cursed inwardly. *Cheap chickenshit boots!*

Her face was just inches from his cock as he ejaculated over it. Hatred mingled with desire in an excruciating moment of pleasure and left him on fire, tingling, burning as his heart hammered, his ragged breathing keeping time, fuelling him with much-needed oxygen. He'd always held his breath in check during the act. The lack of oxygen seemed to heighten the experience for him, and he recreated the method in his solo activities. He often wondered what it must be like to play for the ultimate stakes – getting trussed-up, suspended with a ligature around the neck, an orange to bite down on ... He pushed the book away. 'Jesus, I need a woman,' he whispered. 'I'm comin' for ya.'

He fell asleep.

As Miller approached the entrance to the club, his ears detected the first strains of a familiar tune.

He greeted the gorilla on the door, raising his eyebrows. The man-mountain mirrored him, his own brows lifting without losing the scowl on his face. The smoke hit him harder than the first time around. The club was still packed. He couldn't believe his ears as he bulled through to the makeshift stage. A female voice sang soulfully, accompanied by acoustic guitar. He pushed to the front. A sense of surreality struck him.

In the glare of the hastily arranged floodlights, a quartet had formed. The singer was the flamenco dancer from earlier. Carla swayed in her seat, miming along to the words of a Gerry Rafferty song: '... another year and then you'd be happy, just one more year and then you'd be happy, but you're crying, you're crying now ...'

There were now two guitarists. The new one, a mulatto, wore a Jimi Hendrix wig. The blind man stood elevated, raised up on a soapbox; he drew a prolonged gulp of air through the side of his mouth. Miller stood in awe, as smoke from his immediate proximity seemed to siphon into it. Tipping back, pointing the horn of his sax at the ceiling, he blew a solo rendition far more powerful than that of the original. The crowd went wild.

Carla stood clapping vigorously and did a little drunken jig. Miller thought his ears and heart would burst. Gathering breath for his finale, sax man handed over to the Spaniard's gentle strumming flamenco and the woman sang the last few words, '... you're going, you're going home...' Jimi launched into a blistering solo. Amid a crescendo of electric and acoustic guitars, sax man blew again to tumultuous applause.

Miller gripped her upper arm gently. She looked startled. 'It's OK, it's me,' he said directly into her ear. 'You look like you've been enjoying yourself.'

She wore a triumphant expression. 'I asked them if they knew Baker Street, an' bloody hell, did they ...' She squinted at him through heavy-lidded eyes. 'Where the hell have you been?' she demanded.

'Making sure he follows us.'

'Are you *crazy?* We need to get away from him ...' She wagged a finger at him. 'Besides, when he sees what I've written about him, he'll come after me to England anyway. That's what I want.'

Miller flashed the red marker pen at her. 'I think he'll be keener than ever to catch you before you get back now.'

'Oh?' she queried.

'Oh, yes,' he said. 'I've written on as many posters I could find – a message for him.'

'A message ...' she said. 'What bloody message?'

'See page seventy-seven, you paedophile.'

She nodded and then shook her head. 'Mmm, clever ... although it doesn't say that anywhere. I'm guessing if he hasn't got the book already, that'll be enough to persuade him to buy it, but how do you know he'll see it?'

'Is the Pope Catholic?' Miller said, as he took her hand. 'You're drunk.'

Catching the disapproval in his eyes, she said, 'And stoned. Well, what did you expect?'

He pulled her towards the door. 'Come on. Let's get out of here.'

Out in the alleyways and side streets, Miller's awareness was on high alert. He sensed no danger, but he couldn't trust his faculties any more; he felt like he had a loose connection.

'The car's just round the corner,' he told her.

'Where are we going?' she asked.

'North,' he said, and opened the door for her.

She snuggled down into her seat. 'Wake me up when we get there,' she mumbled.

He glanced at her; she hadn't put on her seatbelt. Not wanting to debate it with her, he leaned over and pulled it around her, clipping the buckle together. He took from his pocket the phone charger he'd bought earlier, first plugging it into the cigarette lighter and then connecting the handset. He started the engine and pulled off into the night. Once out of town, an inky blackness surrounded them. He drove on, a pocket of light holding darkness at bay.

Carla slept for two hours straight before she stirred, yawning and stretching. She smacked her dry lips, moistening them with her tongue. 'Eeeww! My mouth ... you didn't piss in it while I was sleeping did you? God, I need a wee.'

He looked at her with disdain but, before he could answer, she exclaimed, horrified, 'Oh my God, I think I'm going to be sick!'

He pulled in at the side of the road. She leaned out of the door, retching heavily, succeeding only in dispelling air.

'Feel better?'

She sucked in a deep breath and blew out her cheeks, exhaling slowly. 'I think so. Jesus, remind me not to drink on an empty stomach anymore.'

Pulling away again, Miller let the windows down. The warm night air carried in a sweetness for him, and something that turned into bitterness for her.

She cried softly.

Although he felt her pain, he left her alone with it.

After a while, she turned away from the window. 'I guess you're driving up to Tangier,' she said.

'We've got about six hours on the road left. If we switch driving ...' he questioned the wisdom of his statement. 'I think we might be better off finding somewhere around halfway. Casablanca. We could stop there.'

She turned back to the window, the breeze tugging at her spiky hair. He didn't see the glimmer of a smile that momentarily lit her face.

'I like Casablanca,' she said.

'You've been there before?'

'No, but it looked lovely in the film. I hope we're going to stay somewhere nice ...' she said dreamily.

'With you looking like a Berber? I hardly think so,' he harrumphed.

Sitting up, she looked down at herself and then, looking at his valise on the back seat, she said, 'What have you got in there?'

'Nothing that'll fit you.'

She reached over and grabbed the bag.

'Carla, there's nothing, I'm telling you.'

She pulled out a plain white short-sleeved shirt, lifted the robe, and pulled it over her head. He averted his eyes. She put on his shirt and tied it in a knot at the waist.

From the corner of his eye, he saw the smooth contours of her legs stretching into the shadow of the footwell. 'I didn't bring any trousers,' he said.

'That's OK,' she said breezily. 'I have my own.' She unrolled the pair that she'd stowed in her bag at Mohammed's apartment.

'The one thing I don't understand is why you don't outwit him, using that thing of yours ...'

'It doesn't work like it used to, it seems. It's all a bit haywire. But pretty much, there's only one person I know who can do that, and she's not here.'

She seemed to sober slightly, becoming serious. 'Have you heard anything about the Sister?'

'Not a thing.'

'Another story of mine you ruined. Didn't you think it odd ... her going off with Kale like that?'

He shrugged. 'If anyone knows what she's doing, she does.' His brow furrowed. 'I *know* she's OK though.'

'How are you planning to get me out of the country?'

'I have friends in Gibraltar. If I can get you over there, we can get you home quite easily.'

'I'd love to know how you plan to do that,' she said.

'You'll find out soon enough,' he said.

'God, my arse is turning square in this seat. How much further?'

He glanced at the clock. 'Maybe half an hour. Do you want to stop?'

'No, keep going. I'll do some seat exercises.' After a few repetitions, she put her hand on his thigh. 'What about you? I bet you could do with some exercise.'

He lifted her hand and moved it back over to her side of the car.

On the third choice of hotel, Miller changed tack, much to Carla's delight. He went upmarket, reasoning that the most expensive hotels would be more likely to have a couple of rooms, telling himself it was just for one night.

Dressed as they were, they struggled to convince the mangement to allow them in, but Miller assured them that their clothes had been stolen along with Carla's passport: a problem Miller overcame smoothly with the introduction of several one-hundred-dirham notes into the duty manager's palm.

Carla sidled up close to him. 'We don't need two rooms,' she whispered.

'Carla,' he said, smiling wearily, 'I need some sleep.'

'I'm not tired,' she said.

He shook his head.

'I've never travelled so light,' she remarked as they followed the porter along high-ceilinged, palatial corridors to their rooms.

He tipped the porter, even though he'd done nothing more than show them the way. They hadn't bothered with any conversation, and he'd seemed content with that.

'Look, Miller, there's no way I can go out dressed like this, and I heard you promise the manager we'd be properly dressed for breakfast. Let's go and see what clothes they have for me in that little boutique downstairs, yes?'

'It was closed.'

'I just wanted to look ...'

'We'll go somewhere else for breakfast and see about kitting you out afterwards. I'll see you in the morning.' He turned to open the door to his room.

She stared at him, incredulity plainly evident. 'You're going to leave me all night, alone ... after what I've been through?'

He stopped, thought briefly and then, closing the door, crossed the corridor to join her. 'We'll talk, but I'm bushed, and we've got another long drive in the morning.'

The room was light, spacious and airy and – unusually, from what he'd seen in Morocco so far – it had a wooden floor with colourful and expensive rugs laid out on either side of the bed.

She put her bag down. 'I need to make a call. Is it all right to borrow your phone?'

'Of course it is.' He held it out to her. She took it.

'It's a personal call, is that all right?'

'That's fine, just go ahead.'

She disappeared with it into the bathroom.

'Don't drop it in the toilet,' he called out.

'I won't,' she replied.

He heard her speaking in hushed tones, laughing seductively. He wondered, absently, who it was she was talking to. *I must call Stella as soon as I get the phone back.*

She came out of the bathroom dressed in a white towelling hotel robe, an enigmatic smile on her lips.

'What are you grinning at?'

'I took a picture.'

'Sorry?'

'*Mi lecher*, remember?' She flashed him the photograph on his telephone screen.

He gasped at the sight. 'Wow ... yes I do, but what ... What are you trying to do, Carla?'

'I just need some company. You know, to help me keep my mind off things ...'

'And the photo is a way of reaching out to me, you think?'

Undoing her robe, she advanced on him. 'Well, it'd better be.' She looked more mischievous than ever.

He noticed she had her thumb over the send button. 'Oh, no.' He shook his head, realization turning to disbelief. 'No – don't you dare. She won't believe it ...'

'Are you sure, Miller? Come on, let's have some fun.'

Tiredness washed over him. His resistance was low, but he managed to make light of the situation. 'I'll not negotiate under the barrel of a gun. Give me the phone.' He put out a hand as he moved towards her.

'One more step and I blow this thing,' she said, grinning widely.

'Carla, stop messing about. I mean it.'

She stopped as suddenly as if he'd slapped her. 'You do, don't you? You really care for that girl, don't you?'

'Come on – the phone,' he pleaded.

For a moment, he really thought she was going to send the picture.

She tossed the phone to him.

He fumbled as he caught it. The handset slipped through his fingers, going through one hand, then the other, as he desperately swiped, trying to prevent it hitting the floor. He finally caught it, inches away from impact. He breathed a huge sigh of relief and looked at the screen. The photograph had disappeared. He glared at her. 'Tell me you didn't really have that set to send?'

The expression on her face told him everything.

Twenty seconds later, the phone rang. It was Stella.

'I can explain,' he said gingerly, while Carla fell about, holding her sides.

'Stella, I did not send that shot, she's pranking you ...' One hand covered the side of his face. 'Yes, a joke ...' His head shook vigorously in denial. 'No, I'm not laughing ... *wait* ... Stella!' His eyes hardened as he fixed them on Carla. 'She's hung up on me.'

'Might as well fuck me for real now. She's never going to believe you haven't—'

'Why do you *do* things like that?'

'Well, *some* people like me ...' Tears welled. 'I've been putting on a brave face – can't you see that? I just need you to talk to me. I can't live with what I've done. My ... I'm trying to ... all I wanted was a great story! I didn't ask him to get involved. I tried everything to keep him out.' She shook her head miserably, 'But he wouldn't listen, and I didn't try hard enough.' Anguish was written plainly on her face. She wasn't acting.

Miller knew that, in some ways, she was just like him: basically good, but wired up wrong. She had so much going for her yet was always craving attention in the wrong ways, and never wasted time on the in-betweens.

'Come here,' he said, opening his arms, ready to embrace her.

She shot him a look, anger in her eyes. 'Not in a million years!'

He shrugged. Her ability to turn so quickly within the hardened exterior of her defensive shell revealed a truth about her, one that she sought to hide. She was, beneath it all, vulnerable – yet she'd have everyone believe otherwise. Her balls, her fearlessness, while genuine, were designed to distract from the real her. *Aren't we all like that? Stella and I, always hiding behind something. Miller; just a name, but a brilliant disguise.* For a fleeting moment he felt vulnerable, exposed in the light of his own close examination. He closed it down.

'Well, if you want to talk to me, you know where I am.' He made his way out, down the short passageway, and closed the door behind him.

Once in his own room, he tried to call Stella. She didn't answer. He checked his watch. She wouldn't be in bed yet. *Oh, Carla. The things you put me through.*

He showered and, dressed only in white boxer shorts, slid under the top sheet. Reaching for the phone as an afterthought, he glanced to see if he'd missed any calls. He tapped out a quick text to Stella – *Call me x* – and pressed send. His finger lingered over the menu button. He made a selection and viewed the photograph. With mock disapproval on his face and a cagey smile on his lips, he pressed delete. Within moments, he fell asleep.

He was at the rail of a chugging ferryboat. Sea spray sprinkled his face, the taste of salt strong in his mouth. In the darkness, he saw little beyond the tumbling waves. An unknown darkness beckoned him, and he knew if he followed he'd never return. He wondered if that was how the sailors of old felt, staring out to sea, loneliness conjuring comfort in the form of sirens and mermaids. The wise among them understood the dangers of surrender. *Whom the gods seek to destroy they first make mad.*

A persistent sound filtered into his subconscious, alerting him … gentle but insistent knocking accompanied by urgent whispers. 'Miller, I can't sleep. Let me in!'

He bit his lip and rolled over onto his side.

Chapter 13

A deep throbbing pulsed at the back of his head, drawing him from sleep. Disoriented, he gathered his thoughts.

'What did you kill that kid for, he'd done nothing to you?'

Her! She'd taken to creeping up on him when he was at his most vulnerable.

'He shouldn't have been there,' said Boyle. 'If he hadn't been there, he wouldn't have got killed.'

'Got killed? You said that like it was an accident. Don't you think he lived for a reason after you threw him off the roof?'

He became aware of the muscles in his face pulling expressions that didn't belong to him. Yet he couldn't move. His arms and legs refused to obey him. His mother. She lived on in what little conscience she could find, always chiding him for his misdeeds.

'He should have died the first time. Do you think I wanted to do it again?'

'But you always hated anyone hurting kids—'

'I'd kill 'em!' he hissed through parched lips.

'Judge. Jury. Executioner...' she spat. 'Who gave *you* the right?'

'God, the Devil ... Who cares?'

'Stop acting like your father. It isn't too late. It's never too late to put right wrongs.'

At last, he was able to shrug. The paralysing episodes were becoming more and more frequent. He again cursed the girl who'd almost done for him. 'Eilise. I haven't forgotten about you, what you done to me,' he said quietly. Then, louder, into the darkness of his lonely room: 'I haven't forgotten any of you.' He thought about Carla. She could escape for now. It didn't matter.

He'd cool his heels, return to England, and then he'd put those wrongs right. Numbness crept into his brain, and he lost consciousness.

His eyes cracked open cautiously, and he cursed not having drawn the curtains. The light, and associated heat, forced him to leave his bed when all he wanted was to remain in it for a little longer. He'd move on to another town, give it another week. Then he'd return to England's shores, safe in the knowledge that his Foreign Legion passport and name weren't on the wanted list. To be on the safe side, he'd shave his beloved moustache, leaving his top lip clean. Without it, he'd feel naked and exposed, but it was for the best. He thought about his hair. It wasn't long enough to dye. Besides, he had with him two wigs. He'd use the dark one. It meant he'd have to dye his eyebrows, but that wouldn't trouble him.

Twisting the chair away from the dressing table, he sat down and gazed into the mirror, deep into his soulless eyes, and grinned. The price of love and hate. Maybe he'd even track Kathy down to end her misery. He nodded. She'd like that.

He stretched over to retrieve the book from his bedside table.

'What else you got to say, beautiful?' he said, caressing her face with his fingertip. Opening the book, he found where he'd left off and began to read.

Stella's initial anger had dissipated by the time Miller's text arrived on her phone. She read it and turned her phone off. *Let him sweat.* At the bookcase in the hall, she ran a fingertip along a line of books. There were row upon row of them. Books in the vein of *Supernature,* and *The Romeo Error* by Lyall Watson, Gurdjieff's *The Fourth Way,* Ouspensky, Freud and Jung ... Having worked with a psychiatrist for years, and having scourged her own soul searching for answers, she could see more than a little of herself in Miller. The titles displayed all the signs that they'd been well read by a man seeking answers to himself. Two of his more recent acquisitions sat together in among them. One was a taller volume by comparison, faded from a darker blue with embossed lettering in discoloured silver or palest gold – she couldn't tell: *Mountain Interval* by Robert Frost.

Miller had told her the story behind it. She gently hooked her finger over its top and tilted it. Securing it between two fingers, she lifted it clear. *If a book could tell the story of every hand that had ever held it, what tales would it tell?* She opened the cover and flicked through the pages, preparing to read. A note slid out. On the page it marked was a poem entitled 'The Road Not Taken'.

She read the poem and felt its great poignancy. The irony of it, with regard to her own life, was not lost on her. Understanding that the contents were a personal message, she left the note unread. An image flashed before her of a note left unread for years on her mantelpiece. She'd thrown it away in the end without ever reading it, and yet the contents had been revealed to her by another's voice.

After a moment of further thought, she read the slip of paper.

When I was young, I thought I'd live forever, do something. Now, just waiting for the night to come, I realize that I did nothing with my life. Remember what I told you, boy? You'll know when you find her, that special one, and when you do, no matter what, don't let her go. If things get sticky between you, come and read my book, read my last words. Try harder. If there is another side, I'll be thinking of you.

Sincerely, Douglas Kirk

She wept.

Sliding the book back into the shelf, she turned her attention to the one next to it, Carla's *The Life and Times of William Boule*. Taking it, she wondered what story this hand would tell and if it would reveal anything about the writer that she didn't already know, that she might better understand.

She took it into the bedroom with her, and settled into bed to read.

Given her close encounter with him, it made uncomfortable, but fascinating, reading. She hadn't known he'd been a soldier. He was a hero in an early version of counter-ops, schooled in espionage and surveillance techniques.

No wonder he became a killer. And then Carla skilfully dismantled the vague empathy Stella had felt by revealing that he was a killer before that, giving details of a trail of women who'd inexplicably disappeared wherever he was known to have been.

She revealed that he'd killed his own father – the body recovered from a hellhole known as Devil's Pond – and traced the inextricable links to Miller and the fact that Boyle had been on the ferry on the fateful night Miller's first love disappeared. *No wonder he ran to Carla when she called to say she'd found him.* She laid the book face down in her lap. Her mood elevated. It wasn't about Carla at all. She thought about Ryan, about faith, and fate.

Leaning over the side of the bed, she felt with her hand for the box of Ryan's possessions. Unable to lift it from her semi-prone position, she swung her legs to the floor and crouched, reaching in and pulling it clear.

Never very good at facing up to things, she finally found herself ready to read the last writings of Ryan, found with the letter he'd left for her and Miller. She folded back the flaps and lying on top of everything else was a pocket notebook, the cover a faded royal blue, the top right-hand corner a beige leatherette texture, the pages gilt-edged. It was old. He'd started with the title: *The First Time I Met Vera Flynn* ... She skimmed the passages he'd written. The Sister ... He'd suspected the Sister was psychic, even then.

Winding her way further in, she saw that he'd recorded two predictions she'd made that had come true, and a mysterious third that she'd sealed into an envelope, trusting him not to open it until the time was right.

'But how will I know?' He'd written and recorded her reply: '<u>I</u> will know.'

He'd underlined the first letter of her reply.

He mentioned the stone she carried everywhere, his theories on time and space, chance and coincidence. He concluded that she was already psychic when she came into the stone's possession. She questioned his turn of phrase. It was the other way round, surely?

He noted that while in her presence, others showed a marked increase in psychic awareness, himself included, reporting further that it had dissipated when he no longer saw her.

It became clear that what he'd recorded in the pocket book was intended to be expanded upon at some point in the future. Then she found a page headed 'Bruce Milowski'.

She read with increasing interest. A lot of it she'd picked up when she'd read his official file just before Ryan had died. He'd used Vera Flynn as an aid to his psychiatry, cutting to the core of disturbed young minds, enabling him to speed up the healing process. Young Bruce, now known as Miller, had been next in line to receive her attentions. Experimental ... cutting edge ... her eyes flew over the pages. Bruce had never gone to see Vera, his appointment with destiny deferred until the future. More theories ... Bruce was already psychic, possibly as a result of genetics. She didn't want him healed, Ryan had noted, she had another purpose for him ... but what?

Stella reflected on all that she'd read that evening. The note that had fallen from Kirk's old book, its message appearing connected to her doubts ... for a fleeting moment, she thought she understood how it all came together. *It was engineered, meant to be. Can that be right?* With her question, clarity disappeared like smoke in a mist, leaving her with a tantalizing aftertaste. *I'm a part of it, too. What unseen hand led me to pick up those books?*

She swapped Ryan's notes for Carla's book, and resumed reading.

Stella turned the phone over in her hand and, expanding the photo to its full extent, scrolled down the creamy flesh from the woman's navel and analysed the letters forming the vertical tattoo. *Mi leche.* Her schoolgirl French translated it into milk me but, unsure, she Googled it. *'Lick Me!' The dirty bitch!* She shuddered at the thought of Miller and Carla yet, at the same time, wondered if perhaps she herself wasn't interesting enough. For a moment, she envied the reporter's ability to drift in and out of other lives without attachment, without conscience. *That was it.* The reason she could never be like Carla. She cared too much for people. It made her weak by comparison, predictable. A smile curved at the corner of her mouth and lit her eyes. She knew what she had to do.

At the Google search box, she typed: *Tattooist, Romford.* She selected one and clicked through to its website. She didn't want to emulate her rival's explicit branding, merely express her femininity in a more interesting way.

She'd have an eagle and a dove inked into her skin in the morning.

Chapter 14

Lieutenant Mustafa Mohand had barely got into the station when one of his colleagues called out to him. 'Hey, lieutenant, you picked the right day to visit your mother. All hell broke loose here yesterday.'

Mohand's white shirt was damp with perspiration and he smoothed the creases from it, careful not to press too hard or his hands would stick, making new creases. 'What did I miss, constable?'

Hamed quickly brought him up to date and few minutes later Mohand said, 'So, a white truck with an open back and French plates? If it's the same one, I have seen the man who drove this.' He pinched the bridge of his nose. 'Yes, and on my way in this morning ... I've seen him again on the wall. On a poster ...'

'I've seen those, too! Who is it that puts those up? They're everywhere!'

The lieutenant frowned, knowing instinctively there was a significance to the appearance of the posters, but unable to make a connection. 'Hamed, come with me.'

The two men walked from the station together. On the corner opposite the store where Mohand had first seen the man, someone had scrawled graffiti across the poster. The resemblance was so good; he couldn't believe he'd not realized it was him before. The *pugiliste.*

'It is him, Hamed. I saw him in Ali's shop over there, buying a book. Come, let's go and see Ali.'

'Yes,' said Ali, turning the book over. 'It was this lady. She came and asked if she could sell her book here, C-A-R-L-A Black.'

'Wait,' Hamed said, grabbing at the book. 'Carla Black, she's the woman we're looking for from the hotel ...'

'Now we know what she looks like, we'll find her. Can you read English, Hamed?' Mohand asked.

'No, I can't. Do you want to read this book?'

'Ali, do you know anyone who can translate this for me?'

The lines in Ali's forehead deepened. 'From English to French, maybe. You know the American woman with the red hair, who lives near Ecole Primaire Oued Eddahabmore?'

'With the red hair? I know her. She isn't American, she's a German lady.'

Taking the book with him, Lieutenant Mohand assured Ali he would return it.

'Hamed,' he said pointing to the poster, 'copy that writing down. Can we find out where this woman lives?'

'I know where she lives,' Hamed said.

Mohand raised an eyebrow in his direction.

'She's a teacher at the school ...'

'*Bonjour, Mademoiselle*,' the lieutenant said as a woman with hair the colour of burned oranges opened the peeling, blue-painted door. 'I wonder if I may beg your assistance in translating some English text for me?'

She eyed him suspiciously. 'That's all you want?'

'*Mais, oui* ... What else could there be?'

She invited the policemen in and, once inside, Mohand explained exactly what he required.

'Hamed, give her the note.'

The constable handed it to her.

'This word ... it's someone who likes children in an unnatural way,' she said.

The two men exchanged glances.

'*C'est impossible*!' Mohand exclaimed. 'This man is a *pugiliste*.' He pulled his nose across his face. 'He has many fights ...'

She shrugged. 'You asked me what it means, and that's what it is. Pass me the book, we'll see what page seventy-seven says.'

After locating the page, she read it and then told him what it said.

'It says nothing about children. There must be more. Can you translate the whole book for me?'

'This is about four hours to read, and translate as well, is a big job.'

'I just want to know what it says. Can you read it to me in French?'

'Yes, but you understand, I must charge for my time.'

Lieutenant Mohand picked up a piece of hash from the table. 'You understand this is not allowed for foreigners?' he said, with a hint of irony in his voice.

Knowing full well the penalties, she stared at him. 'You want me to start now?'

Mohand sent Hamed back to the police station; he couldn't see the point in two of them sitting on their hands while she read to them.

'What is your name?' he enquired.

'All my friends call me Rusty, because of my hair.' She pinched a few strands of the deep-flame-coloured hair together, and raised them to eye level, before dropping them.

He indicated the book. '*S'il vous plait* ...' Although he'd have much preferred a written translation, he didn't have time. While she read, he took notes.

She took a break only twice, for coffee and cigarettes. He declined her offer of both, but accepted a bottle of water.

He studied her face as she read on. Around halfway through, the expressions she pulled reflected her discomfort at the content she was relaying, and it occurred to him that the effect on her was doubled by the translation. She was getting it twice over.

His interest piqued as pieces of the puzzle came together for him. Missing women, wherever Boule was known to have been. Schooled in espionage. He was effectively a spy. A master of disguise. Every year, for years following the music festival, they'd received enquiries from Interpol relating to young tourists who'd gone missing. Mostly they were young women. But he would have seen him if he'd been to Essaouira before, surely? Not if he was in disguise.

At the end, Rusty flicked back to the first few pages and studied them closely.

'What are you doing?' he enquired.

'It says this is a work of non-fiction ... Inspector, you've got to catch this man!'

Retrieving the book, he thanked her.

She followed him to the door.

He paused before going out, asking as an afterthought, 'How many languages do you speak?'

'I'm not looking for a job,' she said, laughing. 'But fluently, I speak five.'

He smiled. 'Still, it is useful to know.'

The walk to the station took him ten minutes. Time to think, and compare what he had learned with the facts. The poster. The book. Carla Black. The dead cleaner in her room.

He was popular with the locals, and more people stopped him today than they had done even when they had learned he was about to become a father for the fourth time. It seemed that Hamed had been busy asking questions, and it seemed, suddenly, that wherever he went, everyone was talking about Boule, the man in the poster.

A light sheen of perspiration covered his face as he entered the station. The cool interior and the overhead fans brought welcome respite from the heat. He went into the washroom and freshened his face with two handfuls of cold water. Rinsing his hands, he shook the water from them and gazed at himself in the mirror. One day, he would remove the heavy black moustache that covered his top lip, but not yet. He knew some of the other officers called him Saddam behind his back. One day, he would catch them, bawl them out and then shave it off. The washroom towel was filthy; he never used it, instead dabbing at his top lip with the back of each sleeve, drying the moisture from it and then drying his hands on his trousers – always while performing the ritual he thought of his father. Having watched him preparing for work most mornings, he now did the same things. Staring deeper at his reflection, he shook his head slightly, gently letting the connection to his past go.

He'd had an international criminal at his fingertips, and he had not had a clue. Nothing in the man's demeanour gave him away. Turning his face slightly to one side, he shrugged off the self-doubt that had gnawed at him for the last half hour. Remembering what his father often told him, he nodded silent agreement to the mirror. *Unless you are looking, you do not see.*

Five minutes later, he was in deep discussion with Hamed.

'This woman, this writer ... she was seen with the boy, Mohammed, before the terrible accident.'

'Hamed, if we can believe what this book says, this man is a rapist and a murderer many times over,' he said, pushing the book across the desk, tapping the author's photograph on the back cover. 'And this woman. She writes this book. She comes here putting up posters that do not hang anywhere else but in this town ...' He stopped Hamed's query before his mouth opened. 'I already checked.' He pushed the cover so that it sat squarely in front of the other man. 'Get this picture copied. I want it distributed everywhere. And the poster, get a photo of it and copy that around everywhere. We need to find this woman, and we need to catch this devil before he kills again.'

'I'll do the pictures straight away,' Hamed said.

His eyes grainy with tiredness, Mohand fought against his need for a siesta. More than once, he'd prevented his heavy eyelids from fully closing, but slowly, inexorably, he realized it was a battle he could not win against the habit of a lifetime.

The door burst open.

'Sir, we've had a break. Someone has seen a man matching Boule's description going into a dive hotel in Ghazoua. We think he's staying there!'

'Well, what are we waiting for, Hamed? Let's go!'

Carla's knuckles were poised to knock on the door when Miller opened it. 'Did you sleep well?' he enquired.

'In the end I did,' she said.

Her washed-out expression told him she hadn't. 'Bad dreams?'

'I didn't dream about anything,' she replied in a monotone.

'Oh,' he said.

They walked the rest of the way in silence.

Miller waited adjacent to the foyer, having settled the bill, while Carla spoke to a holiday representative in the reception area.

When she rejoined him, her spirits seemed to have lifted and she insisted that she was going nowhere until she'd kitted herself out in new clothes.

He'd managed to steer her away from the expensive garments in the hotel boutique by explaining there would be a much wider choice elsewhere in town. Time was running out, and the thought of traipsing up and down the cobbled backstreets looking for boutiques that were open didn't appeal to him – and his stomach was grumbling for breakfast.

'That's good,' she said, as she scooted back to join him, full of enthusiasm. 'There's a shopping mall not far from here and we can get something to eat while we're there.'

'Thank God for that,' he muttered. 'Do you know the way?'

'Follow me,' she said.

Outside the streets were already busy, the acrid smell of diesel strong enough to taste. Klaxons blared as surprised tourists rushed clear of what they'd thought were pedestrian crossings. Pigeons pecked at the edge of a path on the outskirts of the human traffic, completely desensitized to people.

They'd only walked a few minutes when Carla declared, 'There it is!'

He couldn't believe what he was seeing. 'You've got to be kidding me,' he said, staring at the huge curved glass and concrete building. 'That looks like something out of Brent Cross ...'

She laughed. 'To me, it's the eighth wonder of the world.'

Inside, the place was teeming with people; the twenty-first century meets the middle ages. The aquarium was among the largest he'd ever seen.

'This is worse than any shopping centre back home. This is like bloody Lakeside crossed with SeaWorld,' he grumbled.

Half a dozen shops later, she finally acquiesced to having enough clothes to last for the journey back to England.

'That's one good thing about losing a passport. You can't get any cash,' she said, giggling. 'I hate the idea of you having to buy me clothes ... Not!'

'I can't believe you didn't bring a cash card.'

'American Express,' she chimed, in her best advertiser's voice. 'You can get money out on that.'

'Not mine – yours,' she said, laughing. 'I seem to have lost mine.'

'I'm having this money back,' he said.

'Do we have to rush off? I love it here ...'

'We've got an hour ... no more than that, and we've got to eat yet.'

'Oh, come on. Let's at least look around until lunchtime, have something to eat and then go.'

'Carla, you seem to be forgetting something.'

'Oh, yeah, that. I don't suppose your budget will stretch to a new iPhone for me? That way I can take photos, and you won't have to worry about lending me yours.'

He looked pained. 'I'm not worried about lending it, because it isn't happening again.'

'Come on, look, over there. I'll pay you back. I promise ...'

Boyle read page seventy-seven. He threw the book across the room, its pages flapping noisily as it flew towards the wall

'Fuckin' liar!' he raged. 'No one knew about that!' Stomping over to where the book lay spread open, spine broken and Carla's image on the back cover facing the ceiling, he slowly and deliberately ground her face with his boot. 'Fuckin' bitch,' he growled, switching his voice, changing it completely. 'I'm comin' to getcha.'

A darkness gathered at the periphery of Miller's vision. A feeling. Something in the air. Like knowing it's going to rain before a storm. The end of his nose tingled and touching it, he felt moisture. He looked at his fingertips. They were smeared with blood.

'We really need to get going,' he said. 'I've got a bad feeling coming on.'

The expression on her face turned to a mixture of disappointment and concern.

His phone chimed, signifying a message. He checked it. *Stella.* The text was two words: *I'm sorry x.*

'Bad news?' she said, arching an eyebrow.

'If we don't get going now, it could be. Come on!'

Heading up a cavalcade of cars and motorcycles, Hamed drove at speeds that tested the lieutenant's steely nerve; blasting their sirens at intervals, the other vehicles joined in.

'No more with the sirens. Do you want to tell him we're coming?'

'We still have five minutes to go before we get there—'

'Slow down, and no more sirens,' Mohand said.

Once they had the area contained, the team went in through the front doors.

'Is he still here?' Mohand said to the man behind the desk.

'I didn't see him go out and I've been here all morning,' he said, shrugging. 'Apart from when I took a crap ten minutes ago ...'

'Quickly,' Mohand barked, 'before he looks out of the window and sees us!'

The burly owner led them upstairs faster than he'd travelled on foot for many years. At the top landing he attempted to pause, breathlessly fumbling with the keys, while the tide of police officers behind pushed him on towards the door.

He knocked. No reply.

'Get that door open!' Hamed cried, fuelled by adrenaline. Anxious looks passed among the men as the hotelier hastily unlocked the door. The officers surged forward.

They didn't have to search the room.

'He's gone,' Mohand announced, wrinkling his nose at some lingering odour and dashing across to check the windows, he looked down. No sign. His men entered the alleyway from both ends, converging in the middle.

Turning away, he noticed Hamed had picked something up from the floor, something which he recognized straightaway. The book. The reporter's photograph on the back had been defaced almost beyond recognition. 'What's going on here?' he said quietly.

Someone outside shouted an alert, and others quickly joined in. He rushed back to the window, looking down again. His men surrounded a large refuse bin; its lid hung down, revealing the body of a man, crammed head first into it.

There was no doubt in his mind who was responsible.

Moving away from the window, he crossed the room rapidly on his way downstairs, speaking to Hamed as he went. 'We need all ports alerted in case he tries to leave the country. Get those photographs of the poster out to them – and the woman – I want to speak with her, too. Do it now.'

The powerful motorbike cut through the air as he left the outskirts of town, the drag pulling at the rider's chest despite his aerodynamic position. The dark tinted visor of the shiny black helmet was open a crack. Riding low, kitbag strapped beneath his belly and against the tank, the wind passing over him made his leather Stetson flap up and down, slapping him like a cowboy riding his back, as he touched speeds in excess of a hundred miles an hour.

In his aching head he struggled over and over with the same calculation, never getting the exact answer, but knowing if he travelled twice as fast as she did, he'd be in Tangier in half the time.

He opened the throttle, increasing his speed.

Chapter 15

Carla hadn't spoken since they'd resumed their journey. Dressed once more in Western clothes, she sat with the robe Mohammed had lent her folded on her lap. The iPhone she'd coerced Miller into buying, still in its box, was in the car's centre console.

From the corner of his eye he noticed her studying the fabric. She appeared to be deep in thought. He respected her need for silence. She'd talk when she was ready.

She sighed deeply and turned towards him, her right shoulder resting against the passenger door.

He looked grim. Subconsciously, she mirrored his expression. She sensed he wasn't telling her everything, but she had things on her mind that she needed resolving, so she snuggled into the seat and closed her eyes.

A few minutes later, exasperated at her inability to nod off, she exhaled loudly as she wriggled upright.

He broke the silence that hung between them. 'Are you OK?'

'What do you think?' she said hotly. 'Of course I'm not OK!'

'Talk to me,' he said, gently.

She took a deep breath, unsure where to start. 'How long did it take you to get over your tragedies?' she said.

'A lifetime ... and I'm not over them. I'm just able to function better, that's all.'

He recalled how it felt some days. The crushing unhappiness he used to push aside, leaving it to destroy him another day. It had grown to the size of a nuclear bomb before, with help, he'd managed to defuse it. Now it lay at the back of his mind, disarmed, a component missing. He wondered absently whether that was the real reason he'd been stripped of his sensitivities. The two went hand in hand.

Carla's voice drew him away from his thoughts. 'It didn't really take you all that time to function properly again though, did it? I mean, after the initial shock ...'

'If you're anything like me, it'll come at you in waves.' He took his eyes off the road briefly, and looked at her face. 'I don't think it's fully sunk in with you, yet. You're in shock, only you don't know it.'

'But I do know it. I've got a story to write and I haven't been able to make any notes since it happened.'

'You know what, Carla? You must be one of the most self-centred people I've ever met.'

'Yes, I know. It sounds bad, doesn't it? But it's how I keep my mind off things ... You didn't help me when I needed you, did you? Mr High-and-mighty.'

'Hey, where's all this coming from?'

'You don't know? Mr I-know-bloody-everything. Jesus!' She clenched her fists, and they trembled as she fought to contain herself. 'What's wrong with me? I shouldn't be like this.' And then she wailed, unleashing her pain.

The cry cut right through him. The vocalization of her agony was heart-rending and drew him close to the edge of his own volcanic suppression.

He wanted to blow, for both of them, but he did what he always did. Taking a deep breath, he disassociated. 'Like I said, you're in shock.'

'Tell me something I don't know!' Tears spilled from her eyes and anger filled her with spite. 'Don't just state the obvious all the time. You know what you are?'

He had no time to respond.

'A bloody cold fish! You could have helped me last night, but what did you do? Pushed me away, that's what you did. A friend in need is a friend indeed ... Did you never hear that saying before? I needed you ...' her words petered out as she ran out of steam.

'Carla,' he said, quietly. 'If we're going to get through this, you've got to pull yourself together, because if you don't – either Boyle will get you, or the police will.'

She turned to face him. 'Get me? What about you?'

'No one knows I'm here, apart from you and Stella.'

Her head dropped into her hands and she covered her face. 'Every time I close my eyes, Miller, I see him there – mangled because of me.' She shook her head. Slowly, voice subdued, she continued, 'You didn't see it. You don't have a clue.'

He placed his hand on her shoulder. 'I was in a taxi with his father ...'

She sat up straight. 'How do you *know* that?'

'There was a time I thought I knew, but now I'm not so sure that it's me who knows. I'm beginning to think I'm just a conduit for someone else's life to pass through ... but I felt it, his pain, a few minutes before he discovered it was his boy in the accident.'

'Jesus ... I'd forgotten you could do that ... Couldn't you have warned him, Mohammed I mean?'

'If I could have,' he said thoughtfully, 'don't you think I would have?'

She stared through the windscreen at the road ahead. 'Are you going to get me away from him?'

The heat of his desire for revenge flared briefly, matching her all-consuming pursuit of the story. 'I'll do my best, but for now, we've got miles to go. Tell me about your childhood.'

'You make yourself sound like a shrink asking me that,' she said, shrugging, 'but why not?' After a moment of contemplation, she continued. 'I've always been driven. Some people would call it selfish. Hmmm, maybe it is. My dad was in his late forties and on his third wife when I was born. Mum was twenty-one. I don't remember much about him from when I was a little, little girl. He was a journalist, a war correspondent. Always away ... reporting on someone else's turmoil. It's funny, when I look back I think it was just an excuse to avoid living his own life.'

'I think a lot of people do that, avoid facing up to things.' The irony of his words was not lost on him. 'What was his name?'

'It was Henry,' she whispered, as though betraying a secret.

'Henry Black,' he repeated slowly.

'Did you know him?'

'No, no, the name sounded familiar that's all. Probably just the connection with you ...'

'There was always a big fuss whenever he came home. Like he was a soldier or something. He'd been injured covering the Korean

War. A piece of shrapnel tore through his lower calf. Left him with a limp, but never stopped him from doing his job. Wherever there was a story to be had, he was there. Anyway, I was twelve or thirteen when he finally came home. Mum said he'd changed. I wouldn't have noticed, but she said it was because he'd had to take a boring job working on a local rag.' Distant memories defied focus. Hazy, and too few to retain a sense of sharpness, they centred around the clatter of typewriter keys coming from behind a closed door, the whirr of the carriage, and the whine of the rollers as each rejected sheet was torn from the machine. But what she remembered most clearly was the silence ... tense, ticking moments, waiting ... and then the sigh of relief from her mother when the keys resumed their rhythm, the bomb disposal unit in his brain having bypassed his short fuse.

'Carla ...?'

'Oh, yes, sorry ... I drifted away. He began drinking heavily and he turned from being the dad I barely knew, into a stranger who criticized everything I did. No matter how good my school reports were, they were never good enough. He always demanded high standards whenever he was home, but he got ridiculous. This sounds awful, but I began to hate him. My hormones were all over the place, he was caustic and abrasive and that was it really. I made my mind up. I was never going to be like him if I had kids.'

'You spoke of him in the past tense. I'm assuming that's because he's no longer with us?'

'He should have been the most important man in my life, helping me prepare ... Oh, I don't know, the more I think of myself, the more I realize I've grown up just like him. How does that work?' She searched his eyes for an answer.

He met her gaze. 'It's hard to say, but sometimes we recreate environments we knew when we were kids, either to feel safe, or maybe work through them ... Tell me something –you said he was in Korea?'

'He was.'

'Did you ever talk to him about those days?'

'How strange.' She shook her head. 'That's about the only thing I ever did discuss with him, before he died. He was telling me there was something he regretted, and I thought for a minute he was going to say ... that he wished he'd got to know me better, but it wasn't that. It was that he'd missed out on a big scoop. He'd bumped into a veteran of the Imjin River campaign, one of the Glosters. The Chinese captured him and brainwashed him into thinking he'd escaped, and planted all these other ideas in his head—'

'Wait a minute,' Miller said, 'did he tell you his name, the veteran?'

'Yes, he did. It was a guy called Wilson. Dad spent years trying to track him down, to get the full story; he interviewed countless vets trying to get more to go on, without success. It was his Holy Grail. Why do you ask?'

'No reason.' Miller couldn't help wondering if Henry Black had interviewed his old schoolteacher, himself a veteran of that battle, himself an escapee from Gloster Hill. And if he did, would the teacher have told him anything?

'You should have been a shrink,' she said. 'You've got me thinking about things differently now ... Not sure if that's a good thing, but what about you? I've never heard you talk about your parents.'

His voice sounded distant. 'I went through a phase where the people closest to me always seemed to die, for one reason or another, and I just felt if I never spoke of them, whatever it was that dogged me might just fail to notice how much I cared, and from there I just got into the habit of keeping quiet about them. Anyway, this isn't about me. It's about you.' He turned his face towards her, his expression an apology for his next question. 'Back in the bar you never finished telling me about the body they found in the hotel.'

'I didn't see it. I tried to get back to my room. After Mo ... before he told me it was the cleaner. Sorry, I'm a bit confused. He told me Boyle grabbed him and threw him off the roof.'

'How did he survive that?'

'He did that free-jumping thing a lot of the kids do. He scraped himself quite badly, but survived.'

Sensing she was on the brink of falling apart again, he said, 'We're not going to have much chance of getting you out of the country in the boot of the car. If we go to the consul you'll be arrested, but you'll have the chance to put your side ...'

Steely resolve returned to her voice. 'Miller, I need him to come after me, or all this has been for nothing. If I get detained, and they catch him first—'

'You won't get your story.' *And I won't get what I want either.* 'Then we'll have to get you a passport another way.'

She arched her eyebrow quizzically.

'The backstreet boys. Chinese, Pakistani ... When we get to Tangier, we'll get it sorted. It'll cost a few grand, but you'll pay me back.'

'How long will it take?' she said.

'I don't know. A couple of hours, if we're lucky.'

She turned, leaning more comfortably against the door, and sighed, 'I'm just going to rest my eyes.'

Chapter 16

The motorcyclist noted that the road was far busier than it had been when he first drove down. Passing the wreck of the garage he'd destroyed a couple of days earlier, he pulled back on the throttle and roared past without a second glance, ignoring the taut lines of police tape twisting in the breeze.

He rode recklessly, timing overtaking manoeuvres to perfection, to the accompaniment of horn blasts all around him as the bike thundered on, slowing only when passing through towns. Attracting unnecessary attention was the last thing he wanted.

The throb of the engine beneath him turned the headache into a thudding drum roll, sweetened with a fiery pain that travelled down his spine and united with nerve centres in his lower parts; the need to urinate joined in, enhancing sensations that added to his state of excitement. Images of women he'd known flashed across the screen in the cinema of his mind, and he was lost on autopilot, until it reached an intensity he'd not experienced on a motorcycle before.

'Fuck it,' he muttered as he ejaculated. He needed a woman.

His tongue flicked over dry lips. His mouth was parched. The dull pounding returned and encircled his skull. Although he hadn't urinated in hours, he knew he needed water to top his system up. His stomach growled, reminding him of the need to eat. He had to reach the port before she did, and snatch her away before anyone realized what was going on. He reasoned that she was either in a taxi, or she'd managed to hitch a ride.

He'd find time to eat once he'd caught her. A tiny seed of doubt nagged at him. *You've already missed her, boy.*

The words only succeeded in driving him on. *You're wrong about that, Dad!* The police would know who he was by now, thanks to that bitch, but they'd not stop him. It was shit or bust. To feel the full heat of satisfaction, he needed her now. Later would do, but it wouldn't be the same. He had plans.

He'd been riding for an hour. From the size of the tank and the distance left to travel, he guessed he'd need to stop at least three, maybe four times to fill up. He glanced at the fuel gauge. It registered empty.

On the outskirts of Bouguedra he stopped to refuel at a service station and bought himself a litre of water. He winced, as he attempted unsuccessfully to remove his helmet. The pain in his head had become almost impossible to bear, and he was no longer convinced it was anything to do with dehydration. Breaking the seal on the bottle, he drained half the cool liquid before replacing the cap and packing it away in his bag. The engine started, he pulled out onto the road, keeping to the speed limit until he'd cleared the small town. He didn't want to draw the attention of the police if he could help it. The gendarmerie was a paramilitary force. If they tried to stop him and he refused to comply, they'd shoot him given half a chance.

Opening the bike up, crouching low, he rocketed past a lorry, and twisting the throttle still further, roared on. A mile clocked over on the odometer every thirty seconds. His head pounding again, he dug in deep. *March or die.*

Anger, and thirst for revenge, drove him on at suicidal speeds between towns.

Once he was past Casablanca, the number of native cars heading for Tangier increased, many of them piled impossibly high. Suitcases and other personal effects were secured in all manner of imaginative ways, but mostly with an array of ropes running under roofs, and criss-crossing through windows, anchored to door handles and bumpers.

The vision of a piece of household ware falling into the road in front of him spurred him into overtaking the mechanical camel train of cars, giving them a wide berth long before he needed to.

Racing along the road, through an expanse of desert, his mind switched to Brooks.

What she said wasn't what happened. That fuckin' Brooks, the liar! The fuckin' liar! You're dead, Brooks. Do you hear me? A chorus of voices inside his head joined in. His skull filled with nagging pain.

'You're all dead, can't you understand that?' The sound of his voice startled him. He'd thought he was only thinking. 'Leave me alone!' He spat out the words, but they were deadened by the padding of the helmet.

A mocking female voice sneered his words back at him. 'Leave me alone!'

Boyle surprised himself with the realization that he had uttered the words himself. A pitch-perfect rendition of her voice.

Despite the soaring unseasonable heat, it left him chilled to the bone.

High above, he felt the eye of someone watching him. *A helicopter?* He couldn't hear any rotors above the sound of his engine.

Now nudging one hundred and thirty miles an hour, he didn't dare look up.

Chapter 17

Driving, the lieutenant found, helped him think abstractly. Hamed's voice in the background didn't distract him at all. *A reporter writes a book about a killer. Somehow, she finds out he is in Essaouira. She comes and puts up posters and distributes copies of the book. There are no other posters put up anywhere else in Morocco – Hamed had already checked that. So, why? ... She wants him to find her! He came looking for her in the hotel, went to her room, and the maid disturbed him? Perhaps ...*

His subordinate spoke rapidly, mixing Arabic with French. Mohand's attention switched to the younger man as he queried the radio operator at the other end, 'Then who is he?' he said. 'I want to know immediately there is further development.'

'What was that about?' Mohand asked.

'The body is that of a German tourist, according to his passport, but they can't be sure.'

'Can't be sure? What do you mean?'

'The passport was reported stolen two weeks ago.'

Mohand held the bridge of his nose as if he had a nosebleed. 'What does all this mean?'

'We've learned he was staying across the street from this Boule. We don't think they were connected. It looks as if he was killed for his motorcycle. It's missing.'

'Do we have the licence plate number?'

'Soon we'll know. How can you be so sure this woman is heading for Tangier, lieutenant?'

Mohand's eyebrows lifted, feigning surprise. 'Because she's on the run too, and if she can't get the plane what else can she do?'

'If she's really on the run, she could try a fishing boat ...'

'Hamed, she has no passport. She doesn't use official channels. She was in the hotel. She knows we want to speak with her, no? She is wrapped up in this somehow. I don't know what spider and fly game they are playing, but I have a feeling if I catch her, I'll catch Boule also.'

'You can't go to Tangier, you have no permission.'

'Hamed, what permission do I need? You forget something. I come from Tangier. My mother, she lives there.'

'What about me?'

'What about you?' The lieutenant looked him up and down. '*You* can't.'

'I still don't understand why you'd take such a chance, acting outside your jurisdiction.'

The lieutenant checked the radio was off and, despite the fact only the two of them were in the car, lowered his voice. 'I don't have the proof, only what I feel – here.' He thumped his left breast. 'If I don't act, he'll be gone, and someone else will report their daughter missing. Maybe not here, maybe Spain, or France ... It only takes a few good men to turn their backs for evil to flourish, Hamed'

'This I know, but how will you get the proof, what will you do?'

'The woman. She can help me. Of this, I'm certain.'

'Lieutenant, it's now 14:00 hours, so they have ... we don't know how long ago, but the man, he's at least three hours ahead. You'll never get to the port in time.'

'Didn't I tell you I have contacts? Didn't you think I got to this position because I don't make friends? One such man, he has a helicopter ...'

'He'll fly you there?'

Mohand thought about the years he'd turned a blind eye to the man's illicit selling of alcohol, always turning down the bribes offered, knowing one day he'd call in a favour. 'If he knows what's good for him, he will.'

At some point, Miller couldn't be sure exactly when, Carla's breathing changed, and she began to snore softly.

A yellow light illuminated the tank symbol on the dashboard. *Christ!* He thought quickly; on most cars these days there was at least fifty miles of petrol left when the warning light came on. The last sign he'd seen showed the next town was a hundred kilometres away. He eased his foot off the accelerator, slowing to the optimum fuel consumption speed of fifty miles an hour, and did a mental calculation. *That's sixty miles away.* Unless there was a margin built into the triggering of the light, he was going to be short.

Perspiration sheened his forehead and his palms felt clammy. Vehicles started overtaking, even some of those that were stacked high with belongings.

The brilliant headlights of a motorbike appeared in the rearview mirror. In spite of the daylight, they dazzled him.

'Well, go on then. Overtake,' he mumbled.

A few seconds later, it was obvious the bike was tailgating him. He'd heard about such antics when he'd hired the vehicle. The advice given was to ignore them. Through the glare, he just made out the biker's jet-black helmet. And a hand, finger outstretched, pointing down at the rear, right-hand corner of the car.

Cursing his lack of attention while talking to Carla, he wondered if the rider could see the yellow light, if he knew he was almost out of gas. He dismissed the thought as illogical, but still the bike sat squarely behind. Scenarios played out in his mind. He would run out of juice in a remote place, and if the guy had bad intentions ... He could see that he was big. He thought about weapons. He could pick up a rock, but what if the other man had a gun? Sweat soaked the back of his shirt and then he realized he wasn't afraid ... not for himself. If he'd been on his own, he wouldn't have cared.

'Oh, Carla,' he whispered. 'The shit you put me through.' He glanced in the mirror. The bike roared and swung out, slowing as it came level with his door. The rider's head turned towards him. For an instant, he saw himself and the car reflected in the black visor, and then, with a thunderous burst of acceleration, the biker was gone.

Chapter 18

Hamed had taken over the driving, while Mohand radioed the station to advise that his mother was sick, and it was imperative he left immediately to be with her.

The next call he made on his mobile and, having explained his predicament, the need to get to Tangier quickly, the man on the end of the line agreed to help. 'You're very lucky, Mustafa Mohand. I have one helicopter available immediately. We aren't busy at this time of year. I can make a special price for you.'

'We'll talk about that.'

After a short pause, the man at the other end of the line said, 'I'll have my man meet you at the general air terminal. Sadly, my friend, you still need to check in.'

'No problem.' He ended the call. 'Take me to the airport,' he said.

'You'll fly?' the younger man asked.

The lieutenant looked out of the window, as if seeing his world for the first time lit brightly in the early afternoon sunshine. 'I hope so,' he said with a laconic grin. 'I've never been in a helicopter before.'

'A helicopter?' Hamed chuckled. 'Let's hope the pilot knows how to crash safely ...'

Twenty minutes later, Mohand clambered out of the car outside the airport terminal. After the air-conditioned journey, the heat was stifling. He closed the door behind.

'May Allah be with you,' Hamed called out as he drove away.

Surprised to see Mehmet outside the entrance, Mohand marched up to him. His father's old friend was too busy smoking and thinking to notice his approach. A portly man, almost as wide as he was tall, his head was as big as a football; his swarthy features were anchored in place by the obligatory handbag moustache, surprisingly black, when what little remained of his hair was grey. 'Mehmet, so good to see you again.' They shook hands vigorously.

The lieutenant recalled his father telling him how he had encountered him not long after Mehmet opened his first shop. They'd been friends since school, and while one had chosen to become a policeman, the other had taken his chances, like a dog in the street. He'd shown his old school friend around the modest premises, told him of his plans to make it big one day. For the first time in his life, Mehmet had a legitimate reason to feel proud. After that, they'd met frequently. His father had been astounded at his rapid progress, greased by the elimination of his business rivals, aided by a few well-placed bribes. His father never took any money, but accepted occasional favours. *It is better, my son, for a man like Mehmet to have gained this position than his rivals. For this reason, I turned a blind eye to his activities provided he did not go too far. And besides, sometimes a policeman can use the help of a man from the other side of the law.*

Check-in was a formality, and took place away from the main desks.

Once they'd cleared security together, Mohand enquired, 'Is it possible to follow the line of the motorway?'

'For what?' Mehmet narrowed his eyes. 'We're in a straight line from here to there ... Wait, this isn't police business?'

Mohand scratched at the day's growth of beard on his chin, moved his fingers up to lightly stroke the heavy moustache. Even if he did spot Boule on the motorcycle, they wouldn't be able to land. To be effective, he'd need a ground force. Getting an all-ports alert was one thing: a manhunt, on his sketchy evidence, quite another. 'No, I'm visiting my mother, that's all you need to know.'

Seeing the potential to wriggle out of the expensive favour, Mehmet ventured, 'Rather extravagant, a private helicopter charter to visit mother in Tangier, wouldn't you say? Questions may be asked, and—'

'Who will ask those questions, eh? Let me tell you something, my father's friend, you will have some questions to answer of your own, if I don't get your full cooperation. Do I make myself clear?' He fixed him with a steely glare and jerking a thumb in the direction of the helicopters, said, 'Now, get me up in one of those things. I have no time to lose.'

The rotor blades picked up momentum and the noise, even through the headset he wore, was deafening. Within minutes, they were airborne and travelling north as the crow flies. Mohand leaned forwards and peered down nervously at the ground below. Seen from above, the landscape was predominantly rocky desert, huge barren areas, windblown dunes clearly visible, scarred by deep gulches, pockets of lush vegetation sprang seemingly out of nowhere, scattered, completely out of place, mostly natural, some bordering man-made structures.

'How high are we?' he shouted above the noise.

The pilot turned his head. 'Five thousand feet!'

'Merde ...' he said. 'Seems it's much higher than that.' *Two hours of this noise.* Settling back into his seat, it suddenly dawned in him. He flicked his wrist, at the same time snapping his fingers; the sound drowned out by the engines, the gesture seemed hollow.

The reporter wanted to finish her story! Switching his line of thought, he backtracked. He understood the books and posters had been a ploy to confirm Boule was in Essaouira. He knew from witness statements she'd paid the boy to put up posters. He preened the forest of hair above his lips. *Did the killer see him putting them up? Was that why he mowed him down? No, the porter had admitted he met Mohammed and told him which room the Englishwoman was in. The room they'd found the body of the cleaner in.* He clapped his hands together hard enough for the sound to make the pilot screw his head around to look.

'Excusez,' he muttered, not caring if the other man heard. *Why hadn't he seen it before? The boy saw him. He was a witness. Boule must have seen him.* The pieces were falling into place. *But the boy – why was he at the room and, more crucial to the question, why was Boule there? He had to have located the reporter beforehand. How? Did he follow her? No. If he had, he would have killed her already.*

His head ached, compounded by the beat of rotors and the thump of beaten air. That vein of thought dried up. He shifted. *If her objective had been to just finish the story, at any point, once she'd established his presence in the town, she could have gone to the police.* The revelation struck him like a fist hammering on a door. *She wants him to follow her to England? But why?*

A wave of nausea threatened to engulf him. Airsickness, worse than any he'd encountered before. *Father, could you not have befriended someone who would later charter flights in conventional planes?* His head spun. *How much longer?* He closed his eyes and fought to keep the contents of his stomach from the back of his throat and then, calmly taking a brown paper bag, opened the top and bowed to the inevitable.

Chapter 19

The Vigilante, you say? Yes, I believe I met him. He came here. I'd just finished telling the whole pub how I thought he'd got past a pair of Rottweiler guard dogs before beating the two of those perverts to death – they'd kidnapped a little boy, you know – and I said if I ever met him I'd shake his hand for what he did. In the yard, out back of that farm, the police found dozens of missing boys buried ... If he hadn't stopped them, who knows how many more ...

Anyways, I turned round at the bar and this stranger was there, holding out his hand, wanting to shake. I thought it was just some joker who'd heard what I'd just said. I didn't think for a moment it could be him; I mean, what a coincidence.

I've never shaken the hand of a man with so firm a grip in my life, but he was a good man, I could tell ... Yes, I heard about the young bridey that went missing the night he was in town. Some people think he must have had something to do with it, but to me he seemed like such a good bloke. It makes no sense.

Bryn, regular drinker in King's Head public house

Stella continued the book. Her trepidation grew with every page turned. *Carla, you bitch, what have you got Bruce into?*

She tried calling him to check that he was all right, without success. *It has not been possible to connect your call.* Connection failed? Her heart had picked up a few extra beats. She'd leave it a few moments and then redial, but her finger found the buttons immediately and tried again as if driven by another part of her. *It has not been—*

94

She cut the message off, opened the text menu, and typed. *I love you. Call me. NOW! x* After she'd pressed the send key, she carried the phone in her hand from room to room, forgetting several times what she'd set out to do.

Still no response. Again and again she tried and, in the end, decided she needed to go out.

She took the car.

Without really knowing how she'd got there, she arrived outside Miller's offices. She'd thought earlier about calling in, just to check that no post had slipped by the redirection notice they'd given the postal service.

Pausing in the car for a moment before getting out, she concluded she'd driven on autopilot; a head full of busy thoughts preoccupied her. *How do you do that?* she wondered.

Since she'd persuaded Miller to pursue a career in something less dangerous, he'd put the offices up for sale. Occasionally, deliveries by hand still turned up, shoved into the letterbox. The emails she managed from home; almost everything could be done from there these days. To build a presence on the lecture circuit, maintain the investments he already had, to boost the income pot – it made sense – the offices had to go.

Once through the picket gate she turned to open the padlocked mailbox. She had no need to go inside, but a sudden desire for a warm drink lured her in.

She checked her phone again. Still nothing.

Letting herself in at the front door, the stale odour of abandonment and uncirculated air greeted her. The alarm emitted a series of warning beeps and she rushed to the panel to turn it off. She switched on a large extractor fan, a throwback to when smoking had been allowed in places of work and then, from behind burglar bars, opened a window. It wasn't dark inside, but she felt the need for more light. She flicked a switch, and the dated fluorescent tubes glowed at each end, flickering and popping, until finally illuminating along their whole lengths.

The building had been constructed with security in mind, and the locals knew it. Miller had told her that they'd given up attempting to get in years before. She recalled her original spell of working with him.

Taking a cup from the cupboard, she inspected it for cleanliness. Satisfied, she took a green teabag from its box, and dropped it in. She filled the kettle absently, turned it on and waited for it to boil, the way she had countless times before.

She recalled the first time she'd met him. Her hands had flown up from her lap like two flapping birds when she started to speak; she was so nervous, she couldn't control them, but he'd put her at ease. *How long ago was that exactly?* It seemed like a lifetime.

She'd got the job. Although he'd teased her with parlour games when they weren't busy and she had an inkling he might be psychic – or just very clever – she never had the courage to tell him the truth about her past ... the real reason for taking a job with a missing-persons investigator. She realized she was smiling.

In those days smiles had come rarely – or at least, looking back, she thought they had. *Was he really psychic?* He said he wasn't now. The Sister had stripped him of his abilities. But was he truly, ever?

Once, she recalled, not long after she'd started work with him, he'd told her a story.

'I'd just passed my driving test. I was late taking it compared to the other lads my age – on account of the breakdown I had—'

'You had a breakdown ...?'

'That's something for another time, maybe. I was involved in a shunt accident. The first car stopped suddenly, the car in the middle ran into the back of it, and then I slammed into the back of *him*. It's the only car accident I've ever had. His brake lights weren't working; one second he's going, the next – bang – stopped. We all got out. Middle-man was really agitated, aggressive. It was fight or flight ... he just wanted to get away. Anyhow, the police weren't called, they just happened to be passing, and as soon they'd pulled in, middle-man took off on foot. One of the officers ran after him. It was then we noticed this awful smell coming from his boot. It'd popped open as it crumpled in the collision ...'

Her eyes widened. 'Oh my God, don't tell me! Let me guess ... there was a body in there!'

'Close, but not quite.'

'Well, what was it then?'

'A cardboard box, all done up in string and tape. The underneath was wet and stained with blackish, dried-out tidal marks. The policeman untied the string. The whole thing seemed to be buzzing angrily. As he peeled the last of the tape away from the top flaps, he looked grim. The noise was growing louder. He opened the box and a mass of bluebottles swarmed out, enveloping his head. I can still see his face as he beat them off, all crinkled up in disgust.'

'But what was it?'

'It was a man's head. Full of maggots. Too far gone to be recognized. When they caught the driver, he claimed that although he'd stolen the car, he hadn't looked in the boot, and that was borne out by the fact that a key had snapped off in its lock. Coming so soon after the Olga Kale case, it made my mind up for me. It was what I wanted to do. Solve mysterious cases, and find missing people.'

'Did you solve that one?'

'It wasn't mine to solve.'

'Who's Olga Kale?'

He examined his fingernails. 'Another time.'

'You mean you'll tell me another time?' His demeanour told her nothing. She continued. 'You said you had a breakdown ...?'

'Yes, I did.'

'What sort of breakdown?'

'Does it matter?' He'd put his hands together, fingers and thumbs linked, but held apart, open – a receptacle it seemed, for his thoughts. 'It was all such a long time ago.'

'Tell me,' she said, leaning forwards. 'I want to know.'

He didn't look at her as he avoided the question. She remembered how he'd looked ... she couldn't quite define it. Shame or guilt? She couldn't be sure. She decided not to press him. *Another time.*

She'd returned to her desk. Miller was walking into his office. He closed the door without looking back. She remembered thinking that he would.

She looked down at her keyboard; on it was a folded piece of paper. She opened it. Inside, it said: ANOTHER TIME. Without fully understanding why, she'd tucked the note into her bag.

Later, after work, while in the bath, she stared at the note, holding it out in front of her with both hands. *Coincidence, or what?*

Was she reading some significance into it that wasn't there? Was he telling her something? Why leave a note when he could have just said it. Did he know it was predictive? Was he just telling her, simply, 'Another time.' She drew a mental line. At one end, she had coincidence. At the other – he'd known what she was thinking and, with the note, was just letting her know.

She folded it, and placed it on the rim of the bath.

Afterwards, as she stepped out, a few drops of water from her body spilled onto it, soaking through, distorting the ink, causing it to spread and leach through the paper.

She dried herself and then picked it up and unfolded it. A symmetrical pattern had formed. It looked like a bird of prey.

Slowly, she came out of her reverie. She checked her phone again: still nothing. She'd connected with him before; couldn't she do it again? The tea steamed in her cup. She didn't recall making it. Picking it up, she walked into his office and, placing the cup on the desk, imagined him sitting on the other side. *You OK this morning, Stella?*

No, actually. I've been trying to reach you, and you don't answer your phone ...

Lines of worry furrowed her forehead as she approached his chair. Turning it towards her, she sat down. Placing her phone down on the blotter, she was stunned by what she saw. In among the squares and concentric circles he'd doodled were sketches of tiny eagles and doves.

Her fingers traced the sketches. Doodling. She knew something about it because not long after she'd gone to work for Dr Ryan, he'd noticed her scribbling abstract designs on a pad while on the telephone, in the middle of placing an order for stationery. He'd said it was an unconscious aid to memory, a means of holding focus without slipping entirely into a daydream. Strange, but she remembered what the woman on the other end of the line had been checking was in stock. Lead refills for Ryan's beloved vintage silver pencil. Her own subconscious drawings included rippling pools of concentric circles. She was almost in touch with that one –

the effects of a stone dropped into a pond. Others: flowers, circles, tubes, eyes ... She then remembered Ryan lifting the pad to get a better look at what she'd sketched, and his brief interpretation of them. *These sketches are typical of those who are always searching for love, for meaning ... for themselves.*

She hadn't asked him to elaborate because in her heart she knew what he said was true. *Why an eagle and a dove?* She imagined he was the eagle and she was the dove. Fanciful, perhaps, but possible. She wondered what Ryan would have made of it.

Her mood swung between absolute faith in Miller, and the seed of doubt sown by the receipt of the photograph.

Time passed. The longer it went without a response from him, the more the seed grew.

She put her fingers and thumbs together, the same way Miller had when he'd given her the note, remembering a theory he'd passed on to her about churches and steeples – how the collected consciousness was gathered, and then funnelled up and out into the ether by the shape of the spire. A giant radio transmission aerial. It occurred to her that she'd arranged her fingers in just such a way.

'Ridiculous!' she said aloud, but concentrated anyway.

Chapter 20

For the last ten miles Miller had expected the car to suddenly die on him. It seemed he'd counted every single yard. To squeeze out extra distance he'd turned the air conditioning off. Despite the windows being open, the interior of the car was very warm. He very rarely broke sweat. His mind travelled back in time.

His old teacher, Kirk, had awakened an interest in Middle and Far Eastern thinking in him. There was Tumo, the generation of heat, the meditation on inner fire. He'd learned how to do it, and by visualizing snow and ice, he could achieve the reverse. This time, his thoughts hampered by anxiety over the car running out of fuel, he'd been unable to attain the correct state of mind. What he noticed, more and more during the last few miles, was that he couldn't get Stella off his mind.

'Carla, check my phone will you?' Tensions had been high between them; she was uncomfortably hot, much more so than he was.

'How much further to this bloody garage?' she said, a spike of irritation in her voice.

The rushing breeze and steady rumble of the tyres on the road made it hard to hear. 'Just a couple of miles more. Will you check my phone?'

She twisted in the seat to face him. 'Problems?'

'I haven't heard from Stella for a while. With the noise from the windows, I can't tell if it rang ...'

Carla checked it under his watchful gaze. 'Nothing,' she said, and joked, 'You're obviously out of favour.'

'How many bars? Is there a signal?'

'Yes,' she lied.

'Why did you just lie to me?'

'Sorry?'

'You heard me – why did you lie?'

'If you knew the answer, why ask?'

He sucked in a breath. 'Because when I asked I didn't know ... only after. Your tone of voice gave you away.'

'Do you want me to text her for you?' she asked, mischievously.

'No, just put it down, will you? I'll do it myself when we stop.'

Sing-song fashion, she muttered, 'Pick it up, put it down ...'

'Well, I can't trust you with it, can I?'

'You can trust me, Miller,' she cooed, and reaching over she stroked his cheek lightly with her fingers.

He shied away. 'Don't touch me,' he said.

She let her hand fall, slowly caressing his upper arm, letting it slide lower. 'Are you sure?' she whispered.

He picked her hand up and dropped it into her lap. 'There's the garage,' he said.

Miller pulled in, switched off the engine and instructed the attendant to fill up.

'Oh, goody. Looks like there's a shop inside. I can get out and stretch my legs, go for a browse.' She undid her belt, got out and headed for the building. He checked the telephone. There was only one bar. He tried calling, but couldn't connect. Drafting a quick text, he pressed send, hoping it would go as soon as they passed into an area where the signal was stronger. The heat was stifling in the car; he couldn't wait to switch the air-conditioning back on once the tank was filled and they got moving again.

Paying the attendant in cash, he then decided it would be a good idea to visit the toilets before setting off again. He locked the car and passed Carla on her way back, laden with water and other essentials. He tucked the keys into the fold of her elbow.

'You could have opened it for me ...' she called out to him. 'And if you're going to use those toilets – they're disgusting!'

He continued across the concrete forecourt.

When he returned to the car he wasted no time before resuming the journey. From the corner of his eye he could see her swigging suggestively from a litre bottle of Pepsi, her lips wrapped completely around its mouth. Withdrawing the bottle, she wiped her mouth and offered it. 'Want some?'

'Can't I have my own bottle?' he said.

'Oh, I've put the rest in the boot. Sorry.'

He took it and drank.

'It's like kissing in a way, isn't it? Sharing a bottle like that.'

'Do you ever think of anything else?'

'You know, you're one of a privileged few to have actually had me.'

'Carla, I've known you for a fair while now, and I'm not so sure that's true.'

'I use my body to get what I want, yes, for sure,' she said, indignantly, 'But I don't give it up for just anyone.'

'Oh, come on. You'd do anything for a story.'

'That is so not true. What's up with you, anyway?'

He considered her question. 'I haven't heard back from Stella, thanks to you.'

'Aww, now come on, it was just a joke. You can't blame me if she's overreacted.'

'But I do blame you—'

'What? Because she's blown you out over a silly little joke!'

'No, Carla, she hasn't. I heard from her a couple of hours ago, since the photo. She apologized for doubting me. One thing I can say about her is she's loyal and trusting.'

'So, why did you just say "thanks to me" when you've heard from her since?'

'Because I still can't believe you did that. You're just not rational. I mean, all that fuss about needing a new phone, and it isn't even out of the box!'

'I can't believe you're singling me out for a go after all I've been through.'

He hesitated. 'I'm not, but it's an undeniable fact, no matter how you feel, if you hadn't come here none of this would have happened. You don't think it grants you impunity from the consequences of your actions, do you?'

She turned in her seat without answering, and presented him with the back of her left shoulder.

'Yes, it was unfortunate,' he continued. 'I know how guilty it makes you feel. Believe it or not, I can feel it. But you did come. And I followed. Not for you. For me. Now if you don't mind, I want to think about what I'm going to say to Stella when I can finally reach her.'

'What do you mean, you came for you?'

'Nothing. End of discussion.'

She turned to face him. 'Don't you like me, even just a little bit?' Tears spilled down her cheeks. 'You know I could make you very happy ...?'

'Carla,' he said softly. 'Enough ...'

She shrugged. 'Don't say I didn't try. I still like you. Maybe I even—'

'Enough, Carla!' he said through gritted teeth. 'That's enough.'

After a brief silence, she said, 'I'm sorry.'

He didn't answer. He was in touch with a higher part of himself; he believed what she said was true, but he was now focused firmly on Stella.

Looking out at the road ahead of him, he felt her presence.

Chapter 21

I'd only just escaped from him and wound up at my biological mother's house; it's a long story, but she put me up for the night and the next thing I know, he's got in and was attacking my mum. I battered him with a rounders bat; he wouldn't get off, so I bashed him as hard as I could on the back of his head ... What was it like finding out my kidnapper was my own father? If I'd known at the time all the things he'd done, I'd have finished him off with that bat.

Eilise Stapleton, kidnap victim

The constant drag, the wind resistance pushing against his upper body made his shoulders, neck, and arms ache. His head was swollen. As a fighter, he knew it, could feel it. The pressure of the fluid between his brain and skull increased with every heartbeat, pumped up by every pulse at his temples. His head throbbed as it expanded and filled the entire space inside the helmet. *It's felt like this before.*

Once, some lads had jumped him – more than a dozen of them. The whole thing unfolded like it had been only yesterday.

He'd been approached by a stupid-looking, angel-faced boy who'd said nothing, but cocking his thumb beneath the cigarette dangling from his lips he'd made it plain he wanted a light. He couldn't have been any more than eighteen years old. The rest of the group stayed back, huddled together.

Their faces had given them away. They looked too casual; none could look him in the eye. He reached into his pocket for his lighter with his left hand, knowing what would come, but not caring.

The kid smacked him hard, catching him on the side of his jaw. The boy was strong. It was a good punch, but not good enough.

Retaliation was instant. He butted, his forehead crashing into the bony ridge above the lad's eye, smashing it. At the point of impact, blood welled from a gaping wound.

The group behind opened up as the boy hit the ground.

Stepping over him, he took the fight to them – something they hadn't expected. That was when he saw some of them carrying baseball bats and crowbars, but he'd committed to fight, not run. Fist, boot, elbow and head. Four more went down before they landed a blow on him. It was a coward's strike, just like that of the girl he'd kidnapped, delivered from behind with a blunt instrument.

He hadn't gone down, not at first. Two, maybe three more men had been laid out by his ferocious counter-attack ... another few seconds and he'd have taken them all.

And then it was lights out.

He'd regained consciousness in the ambulance. The medic told him to lie still. 'Your head's the size of a football, mate. You've had a right kicking.'

It turned out he had a fractured skull. The doctor told him it was a miracle he'd survived, and then probably only because he was a fighter and repeated concussive blows had caused the fluid that cushions the brain to thicken, giving him an edge of protection.

The recollection triggered the realization that his ability to think straight had been impaired.

'She broke your head and you never got it fixed,' the voice rasped. 'Serves you fuckin' right after all you've done.'

A flash of blinding pain stabbed his forehead; he felt the skin ruck up against the padding inside the helmet. 'Come to kick me when I'm down, have you? Well, I ain't finished yet,' he growled. 'I've got a job of work to do, and when I've done that, I'm going to fix you once and for all!' He braced himself for his mother to join in. Apart from the rumbling in his head, and white noise inside his ears, there was silence.

That's what she's done, he rationalized, broken the skull – and left untreated, whatever was going on in his head was getting worse. *Fuck it. Shit or bust.*

He'd find a backstreet doctor in England when this was all over. A road sign loomed in front ... came and went: Tangier 150 km. An hour; he'd be there. In an hour.

Carla wriggled up in the seat and stretched her arms out, yawning. 'How much further to go? How long was I asleep for?'

'First question, about half an hour: second ... not long enough,' Miller said.

She checked his face, gauging his expression. 'Don't be like that. I'm worried. What if we don't make it out of the country?'

'Pop goes your pursuit story.'

'I'm not joking.'

'Neither am I.'

'So what am I doing in the car with you, then? You don't want me ... you've made that plain. Why are you helping me at all? Why did you come out here, if it wasn't for any of those things?'

Met with no answers, her deductive reasoning left only one conclusion. 'I thought you were joking before, but you've come here to kill him, haven't you?'

Still silence.

She continued: 'Here, in Morocco? Because you think you've more chance of getting away with it?'

He glanced at her. 'OK, let's put it this way ... the thought had crossed my mind, but if I did that, I'd be no better than him.'

She unwrapped her new phone.

'What are you doing?'

'I'm going to make sure I've got enough charge in this to take photos, that's all.'

The value of her story had just gone up.

Chapter 22

I've compromised myself. I made a few bad choices, did some immoral things, but nothing criminal. I'm stitched up so tight, I can't breathe. I can do nothing apart from disappear for a while. Let things take their course.

Extract from DCI Kennedy's letter dated 3 April 2007

Mohand's inner ear had been disturbed by the helicopter journey, affecting his balance. He'd had something similar once after a choppy sea voyage. Mercifully, the pounding in his head had eased considerably.

Outside the airport, he half-staggered to a bench and sat down in the shade offered up by a short grove of palm trees.

Gathering his thoughts, he unclipped his mobile phone from its holster and called Hamed.

'Lieutenant? I was beginning to think you'd never arrive.'

'Tell me what's happened since I left.' Mohand inhaled deeply. The warm air, tainted with aviation fuel, did little to clear the nausea he felt.

'The stolen motorcycle registration has been circulated. Passport control has been put on alert, but there's official resistance to committing police time without real evidence.'

'I knew that would be so. The commander here in Tangier, his father worked with my father. Perhaps I can persuade him to cooperate with me.'

'And if he refuses?'

'I am already alone. I will remain alone. Unless...?'

Hamed allowed a moment to pass and then said, 'Yes, lieutenant?'

'It does not matter. I will visit my mother ... What about this German? Did we find out more?'

'No, they are still checking.'

'If there is anything, a sighting of the bike ... anything … you are to contact me immediately, Hamed, *c'est bien compris*?'

'Of course, lieutenant.'

Ending the call, he scrolled through his contact list on the phone. Some of his ex-colleagues, from when he was stationed in Tangier, were friends. If his plan worked, he needn't involve the commander at all. His explanation, if needed, would be that he was in town, this situation arose, and he dealt with it, as any officer would have.

He phoned his first choice from the list: Sayeed.

After three rings, his call was answered. 'Mustafa? I haven't heard from you in such a long time, my friend, I swear my finger was on the delete button when you called. How did you know?'

Mohand laughed. 'It is the gut instinct. You know? How are you, Sayeed, my friend?'

'I'm very well.'

'Good, I'm glad to hear it. Look, I need some help. Are you on duty today?'

'Everyone is working today. Apart from Farouk, he is sick with something he ate last night.'

Farouk. He knew him. He scrolled down the list, sure he was on it.

'Why do you ask, my friend?'

He took a gamble and confided in him.

'I'm off duty in an hour. I can meet you at the port.'

'Excellent, Sayeed. I will be there.'

He made his next call. 'Farouk ...?'

Five minutes later, he had another recruit.

He considered his next move. *The port, I must go to the port.*

Boyle's backside joined in with the protestations made by the rest of his body. It had gone to sleep. He tried to move around on the seat of the motorcycle to stimulate blood flow. He couldn't even feel his cock. *Fuck, shit, bollocks!*

'You're fallin' apart boy!'

He gritted his inward-sloping teeth. If he'd bitten someone at that moment, he'd have taken a chunk right out of them.

'Get the fuck out of my head, you ain't even real anymore. I killed you, remember? Buried you in that pond you showed me years ago. Keeping all the others company, that's where you are. Where you belong!'

'But I ain't there anymore, boy! You never read that book properly, did you? They found me when they dredged it, when them kids died. Didn't you know about that? Didn't you listen when I told you not to overfish the same place? Course not, you divvy piece of shit! You went back and chucked me in. Should have stayed away ... me and that Chinese girl ... brought you bad luck. Brought it on yourself, all of it. Don't think I don't hear you blaming me. You blamed me for the death of your mother, but it was you that killed her with your evil ways. I heard you say it. "I'm worse than you, Dad ..." We'll see. I'll be seeing you.'

Did he really just have a conversation with his father? It was all in his fucked-up, broken head. Pieces of bone, forcing their way into his brain, depressing the parts ...

What if my memory goes? Then everything would have been for nothing. What good the thrill, if he couldn't play it back in the cinema of his mind?

He dropped his speed considerably, but still whipped past the slower vehicles, switching lanes constantly as the traffic became denser on the outskirts of town.

As he overtook one vehicle on the inside, he did a double take. A snapshot taken from the periphery of his vision, picked apart and reassembled, flashed a match in his brain.

He slowed down. Looking in his rearview mirror, he was now convinced of it. *Her!*

A dark shadow passed to Miller's right. For a split second, he thought it was an alert to danger, the return of an ability that had lain dormant since the Sister had taken it from him.

A motorbike shot past. The red glow of his brake light caused Miller to touch his own pedal.

The angle of the biker's head indicated that he was looking in his mirror. And then he noticed the cowboy hat gently slapping the rider's back.

Carla had seen him, too. Terrified, she shrank into the seat and whispered: 'Boyle.'

Chapter 23

'What are we going to do now?' Carla spoke in hushed tones, as if Boyle might hear her.

'Keep calm,' Miller reassured her. 'He can't do anything here. We keep going. He can't get us now, there are too many witnesses.'

'What about my passport? How are we going to sort that out with him following right behind ...?'

'That's going to be more difficult,' he said, and flicked his eyes up to glance in the mirror. 'We'll have to lose him.'

'Miller?'

'What?'

'I'm glad to hear you saying "we".'

He didn't bother to answer.

The sun flared, gleaming off the windscreen and preventing him from getting a look at the driver. *A rental car! Should have guessed that was another possibility. The filthy slag probably dipped at the roadside like a prostitute. Good-looking woman like that, it was obvious she wouldn't have had to pay a taxi ride.*

Brief images formed of her opening her legs to the cabbie in exchange for the fare. Swiftly moving on from that, another scene arose in his imagination in which he was the driver who'd picked her up. She got in with him, knowing who he was and not caring, blowing him with those lush lips of hers while he was driving.

His cock throbbed. This was too good an opportunity to miss. He slowed down. She looked out from behind the car window, eyes wide as he raised his visor, showing her his face. Terror or desire?

For the second time on the journey warm fluid dribbled into his pants.

He slowed down and tucked himself in behind them.

'Did you see that look on his face?' Carla said. 'He couldn't have made it plainer what he was thinking.' She shuddered. 'Jesus! I think I now know how Stella felt, when he had her at his mercy.'

Miller shook his head. 'Somehow, I doubt that. She was alone and terrified ...' He flashed back to the scene he'd been met with when he'd burst into the room. Stella tied up and naked, barely conscious, an empty syringe in Boyle's hand ... It was just a few months before, yet it seemed like a lifetime ago.

Why didn't you kill him then, and have done with it? One expertly delivered strike while he had him down and unconscious ... There wasn't a jury in the land who wouldn't have believed he'd acted in self-defence against such an assailant. He hadn't only himself to think about, though. Stella would have died if he hadn't acted when he did, rushing her to the hospital. Things happen for a reason, and sometimes things have to happen no matter what, in order for the next thing to happen.

It was meant to be this way. He was convinced of it.

Carla adjusted the wing mirror so she could keep a watchful eye behind. 'Hey! Where's he gone?'

Miller scanned the mirrors. 'He's on my side. No wait ... What's he doing? He's dropping further back.'

'Look! Up ahead,' Carla said.

At the roadside, the flashing red and blue lights of two patrol cars advertised their presence. Several officers picked out bikers, directing them to pull in.

Further up, two police motorcyclists sat ready to give pursuit, should any rider ignore the request.

They didn't see Boyle for the rest of the journey.

Nearing the centre of Tangier, Miller looked out for a car park, his navigation assisted by Carla's new iPhone.

'Take a left,' she said, glancing from the device in her palm and then out through the windscreen. 'Then the next left. You should be able to park about five hundred yards down.' The maze of side streets they'd wound their way into made her feel safer. 'The chances of bumping into him in this rabbit warren must be one in a million.'

Miller shook his head slowly.

'What? What is it you're shaking your head at?' she demanded.

'I was just thinking about how one in a million chances happen one in a million times, that's all.'

'You really know how to burst my bubble, don't you?'

Completely ignoring her last remark, he said, 'I don't suppose that thing will find us a seedy Chinese restaurant, will it?'

'What on earth would you want one of those for? Top restaurants and hotels, maybe, but phooey if you're planning to eat in some cheap takeaway – you can count me out,' she said, eyeing the run-down frontage of several shops. 'What are they? They've got Chinese writing on the signs.'

'That'll be a start,' he said. 'Let's park up and see what we can find out.'

The inside of the shop smelled of feathers and chickens, old boot leather and something else Miller didn't even want to think about.

Carla stayed close behind as he manoeuvred through narrow passageways formed by parcels, crates, bales, bottles and jars containing herbs and liquids. It reminded him of a pet shop he once used to visit when he was a boy. His friend kept snakes, and once a week they would go together and buy baby mice to feed to them.

An old woman viewed them suspiciously from beneath a traditional hat. She could have stepped straight from a paddy field. She studied him, chewing on what he imagined was probably a betel nut. She called out something he didn't understand. A young man in voluminous trousers and a short-sleeved Hawaiian shirt appeared. His smooth olive skin retained the plumpness of youth, but Miller guessed he was older. His eyes were almost black. He carried himself easily, nimble as a cat. He measured Miller and the hard look on his face softened when he saw Carla. A half-grin parted fleshy lips and the end of his nose dipped slightly as he spoke.

'Can I help you?' he said in perfect English.

Miller explained, establishing a mutual trust quickly, assisted by the exchange of currency.

'I know someone who can help you, but this thing you ask for, it does not come cheap. You have money?'

'I can get it,' said Miller.

'And this is for you, lady?'

'Carla. Call me Carla. Yes, it is ... I've not had a very good time of it ...'

A harsh look from Miller silenced her.

'Come with me.' The young man led them out through the back of the shop into a narrow alley where the stench of rotting food was almost unbearable. They walked a hundred yards before their guide stopped.

'Wait here,' he said and, ducking into a doorway, disappeared inside.

A few moments later he re-emerged. 'You,' he said pointing to Miller, 'come with me. There's a bank, not far away. And Carla,' – he nodded towards an old man waiting in the shadows – 'you go with him. He will begin the work while we go for the money.'

Carla glanced at Miller for reassurance: he nodded.

She went inside.

On the way Miller and the young Chinaman struck up a conversation, speaking in low tones.

'You have a problem with the car. There is a big x-ray machine. Every car goes through. People-smuggling is big from here to Spain. She is Western. Passport for Morocco people is no good. Passport is good for her ...'

'How do they do it? I mean, it'll be good enough won't it?'

The younger man laughed. 'How does he do it? How do Nigerians empty your bank account with just your passport details? Best to say, don't know.'

Within an hour of the money being handed over, Carla was the owner of a new British passport.

'Carla,' said Miller, 'we already knew we'd have to be careful, right?'

She shot him a sideways glance. 'What do you mean? What's happened?'

'On the way back from the bank – and it's really strange how these things happen – I was thinking of Boyle, and suddenly I saw him. I stopped dead as he cruised by on his motorbike. I'd made some small talk with the Chinaman about your predicament.' He paused.

'So, we're back to me, and not us, now?' She arched an eyebrow in his direction.

He continued, 'He was on it straight away, saying, "That's him, isn't it?" I didn't answer. Do you know he offered to fix him for five thousand pounds? I refused, of course. It's funny what a great deal you can have when you truly don't want something.'

'Tell me you haven't paid him?' She looked aghast.

'Don't worry,' he grinned, 'he got all the way down to a thousand pounds, but I told him it's personal and only then did he leave it.'

'You haven't mentioned my hair,' she said.

'What about it?' He'd already realized she'd scraped it back from her face and clipped it.

'The old man, he suggested I do it. He enhanced the photo in the passport to make it look as if my hair was much shorter. I think I might have it done like that ...'

'Do me a favour, Carla. You've got a psycho-killer after you, we're about to attempt to get on a ferry, and all you can think of is your hair?'

'No, actually, you're wrong about that. I was thinking about why you didn't just pay the Chinaman. You don't care about my story; I know you don't.'

'Too right I don't.'

'And you didn't come here for me ... So that can only mean what I said before. You're hoping to kill him.'

They approached the head of the alleyway. Miller held her back, as he looked both ways. 'Come on, quick, let's get back to the car.' He walked briskly. Carla struggled to keep up, her sandals slapping the ground with every hurried step.

After a couple of minutes, she said, 'Can't you slow down?'

'The car's only over there.' He nodded to where they'd left it. 'I'd have thought you'd appreciate the exercise ahead of what you've got in store.'

She stopped.

Noticing she wasn't with him, he turned to look for her. 'Come on, it's just another few yards.'

'What have I got in store?'

'I'll tell you once we're in the car.' He held the key fob out and unlocked the doors as he approached. 'Come on, we haven't got all day.' He opened the door and got in.

She shrugged, walked the remaining distance, and let herself in at the passenger side. 'OK, I'm here,' she said, adding with sarcasm, 'Please don't tell me you're going to use me as bait to lure him into a trap.'

'You know what, Carla?' he said, grinning. 'I hadn't thought about that. I think I could make that work. Let me see: I come along just too late.'

'You'd better not, or I'm not doing it.'

He burst into laughter. 'No, that's not it.' He started the engine. 'You're going in the boot.'

She fixed him with a hot glare. 'I'm not getting in there with these clothes on. They're brand new.'

Miller ignored her muttered protestations as he turned out of the narrow streets, winding his way towards the port.

Chapter 24

The feet of the rider skimmed the road, steadying the motorcycle as he rode slowly among the heaving crowds of people who, looking over their shoulders on hearing the engine's low growl approaching, made way for him to pass.

On reaching the far side of the market, he turned into a suitably deserted street bounded by a high wall at the opposite end.

After a few moments, satisfied it would be quiet enough for his purposes, he parked the bike and stomped back to where he rode in.

He needed infinite patience but time not on his side, and something had to give. A few moments later, he struck a well-aimed blow behind the ear of a passing tourist and dragged him from the main thoroughfare.

No one seemed to notice.

Boyle set to work immediately behind the screen the motorcycle provided. A casual glance would suggest to to passers-by that he was working on the bike. He quickly stripped the hapless man, who was unfortunate enough to be of a similar build to his attacker. Once all clothes had been swapped, Boyle applied the finishing touches. Cramming the other man's feet into his beloved cowboy boots, he hung the leather Stetson from its cord around the corpse's neck. Taking his passport from his kitbag, he slid it into the back pocket of the jeans the man was now wearing. One more item to place on him, then that was it. The final deed.

Although his victim looked nothing like Brooks as a younger man, he projected that image onto him and battered him mercilessly, smashing his face into an unrecognizable pulp. 'You-fuckin'-lied-about-that!' His voice kept low and controlled, he punctuated the words with percussive blows as his fist crashed home. 'What-you-got-to-say-about-it-now-huh?'

At the end of the pummelling, he knew he'd killed him.

He found himself remembering something he'd tried to forget, but that reporter bitch had dredged it all up again.

He was fifteen at the time, already a man. Urges had begun that were not easily satisfied. At first, he hadn't fully understood them. He'd taken instinctively to masturbation, and when that wasn't enough to quell the energies that set him ablaze, he took to running.

Something inside him, even at that young age, had told him that one day it wouldn't be enough.

His father had been gone for days. He couldn't understand why his mother had taken to sleeping all the time.

She'd passed out. A bottle of pills lay beside her.

Already day had given way to darkness and, watching her, afraid she might be dead, he leaned over her and listened, close to her mouth. Warm, shallow breath wafted into his ear. She seemed to whisper. Something he couldn't quite make out. *Was it an invitation?* His cock stirred.

He moved his mouth to her mouth, and he breathed her breath, inhaling it, holding it in like smoke from a cigarette.

He repeated the process, his harelip gently brushing hers.

His hand felt like it no longer belonged to him as it trembled, gently caressing her inner thigh, stroking, lifting her dress, moving higher.

He stopped. *If she woke up ...* He shook her; her head lolled, and she slid sideways.

'Mum,' he said, shaking her again.

As day gave way to night, darkness enveloped his soul.

Drowsily, he'd rolled over onto his back, and then Brooks had banged on the window.

Had he seen? He couldn't have done.

When he opened the door, Brooks glared at him. 'What were you doing with your mother just then?'

He couldn't have seen! From the window he'd looked through the table would have blocked his view.

118

'N-nothing. I-I was t-t-trying to wake her.'

Brooks marched past, looked down at her, and picked up the small brown bottle, and read the label. 'Sleeping pills,' he said. 'Come on, boy, we've got to make her sick.'

Whether she'd overdosed by accident he never did find out, but his mother never took sleeping pills again; nor did she ever sleep in his presence when they were alone.

Had she known?

What Brooks told that reporter was a lie. He hadn't seen anything. *No one knew about that. The liar! No one ever knew about that.*

'You're wrong. You think I didn't know? You filthy little beggar!'

He felt the heat of his mother's breath as it passed over his lips. He pressed them together to keep it from coming out. It didn't work.

Pain scorched the back of his eyeballs like invisible thumbs gouging from inside.

'Nothing happened, you were asleep – you must've been dreaming. I swear on your life.'

'You did that once too often, son, and look where it got me. Inside of you!'

If she *had* known, why hadn't she mentioned it before? It was his dad's fault; if he'd been there, the chance would never have arisen. He was going crazy, and he knew it. What was it he'd read when he was self-educating, trying to make a difference in his life? Those the gods seek to destroy, they first make mad.

Ignoring her voice, he began the task in hand, and made a solemn oath: 'You're a dead man, Brooks, spreading your dirty lies.'

He started the bike, hoisted his victim up and over the seat, and got on behind him. Glancing over his shoulder to make sure he remained unobserved, he held his victim upright in place and, accelerating the bike, reverse-leapfrogged just before man and machine smashed into the wall.

He picked himself up from the ground, knowing he had only seconds before people came to investigate the noise. With great difficulty, and in immense pain, he removed the helmet and swung it face first into the hard adobe surface, above the scar the motorcycle had gouged into it. Although the force split the visor in two, it remained fixed by its hinges, either side.

Pulling the dead man's head forward, he forced the helmet over his bloodied face.

Aware of people gathering behind him he stood up, telling them there wasn't anything he could do. 'Phone an ambulance,' he said, and then repeated the request in French. '*Appelez une ambulance.*'

He scanned their faces. *They hadn't seen.*

He slipped away, his kitbag held tight under his arm.

Chapter 25

Lieutenant Mohand strode purposefully in the direction of the port. The mobile telephone in his jacket buzzed insistently. Mildly irritated that his train of thought had been disturbed, he fished it from his pocket and answered: 'Mohand.'

The voice at the other end spoke rapidly.

He listened intently, and then said, 'Are you sure it is him?' A bittersweet blend of relief and disappointment left him feeling dissatisfied as his former colleague told him that not only had the motorbike registration matched, but also, the passport found on the body belonged to Boule.

'Where are you now, Sayeed?' he said, looking around, checking his bearings. 'That's only two streets away ... I can be there in less than five minutes.'

Mohand forced his way through the crowd into the horseshoe-shaped no-man's-land Sayeed had formed, surrounding the accident. A distant siren blared, the sound getting closer as he took in the scene.

The motorcycle had come to rest on its side; the handlebars had twisted back on themselves. Misshapen and deflated, the front tyre had clearly burst upon impact. Fragments of glass glittered like industrial diamonds, embedded into the adobe surface of the wall by the force of the collision. He imagined the headlight exploding, scattering the shards of glass that now spread over a ten-foot radius, glinting in the sun, forming a rough half-crescent on the ground.

Adjacent to the motorcycle, the body of the man he'd been hunting was kneeling in a grotesque parody of prayer, head pushed up hard against the lower surface of the wall.

Sayeed beckoned him to come closer. 'What do you think?'

Mohand scratched the back of his head. 'It looks like suicide. Why else would he be going so fast down a blind alley?'

'That's what I thought. It does seem strange to do it in this way though. There's no guarantee this would have killed him. And if he failed, he would have been crippled … Maybe it was an accident, he thought he could turn …'

'No, it doesn't make sense. Unless he was being chased by someone. This German he killed – he had friends, perhaps?'

Moving around the dead man, Mohand observed the black helmet almost cleaved in two, the visor split apart. He recognized the clothing: the cowboy hat slung from his neck, the matching boots on feet that appeared to have scraped forward towards the head, before coming to rest, legs drawn up into his body – foetus-like, as if knowing he was about to die.

Vaguely aware of the murmuring crowd behind, he squatted, peering in through the gap in the broken visor. Boule's face was a bloody mess, smashed beyond recognition.

'Is it him?' Sayeed asked.

The lieutenant grimaced. 'I do not think his own mother would recognize him, but he has the clothes, the motorbike, the passport ... Yes, I think it is him.'

Still wailing, an ambulance pulled into the turning, and the crowd parted before it. The two men stood back.

Mohand stepped forward, stopping the ambulance. *Something isn't right.* Returning to the body, he crouched to examine the hands. He remembered the day in the shop when he'd first seen him, the *pugiliste*.

'Wrath'. The tattoo. This man has no tattoo!

Away from the main thoroughfare, Boyle stood in the shadows of a doorway with his back towards the light, and kneeled on one knee while he rummaged through his kitbag. Removing a canvas roll, he undid the securing strap and unfurled it. Inside was an array of brushes, cosmetics, tweezers, scissors and a small mirror. Taking a razor from a separate bag, he looked at his reflection, and then dragged the blade down between his eyebrows, removing all trace of hair. Next, he tore the top from a sachet containing a surgical wipe and cleansed the top surface of his head, wincing as he rubbed over the dished area at the back of it. Two minutes later, satisfied it was dry, he unwrapped a thick latex skull cap and stretched it tight across his cranium. A white lightning bolt of pain shot through his head emerging through his left eye. He squeezed them both shut.

The skin of his face tautened as he stretched the rubber down so that it sat beneath the protuberance at the base of his skull. The pain was excruciating. *March or die.* He could take it. He could take anything.

He flashed back to the shock he felt at the blow that little bitch had dealt him. His knees had buckled to the ground. The will that carried him through many a hard fight had been in him as he'd fought to stay conscious. The pain! And she'd wanted to do him with the bat again and again – and if he hadn't moved, she would have done. *Bitch!* Instinct had taken over; he found his feet and made his escape.

Scrutinizing himself in the mirror, he then put it down and removed a passport secreted in the kitbag's lining. Opening it, he set about recreating the look he'd given himself when the photograph had been taken. The first eyebrow hair he plucked made his eyes water. *Shit!* He debated whether to shave them off and pencil them in. Deciding the effect wouldn't be the same, he endured the prolonged process of plucking, thinning and reshaping them into higher arches formed within the former lines of each brow. Half an hour later, after shaving his moustache, he applied the finishing make-up touches before placing a long black wig on his head. Turning left and right, he admired his handiwork in the mirror.

Finally, he stripped and dressed in the dark floral sarong he'd just purchased, along with flip-flops. He stared at his toes. *Forgot nail varnish!* Then he grinned. *Let's not get too carried away, Willy-Boy!*

'What do you do when all else fails, James?' he said, mimicking an Englishwoman's cut-glass accent.

'Why, Miss Moneypenny,' he said, in his best Sean Connery voice. 'When all else fails, by drawing attention to myself in the right way, I hide in plain sight.'

Once he'd packed all he needed into the large, rainbow-striped beach bag he'd bought earlier, he dumped everything else into a refuse bin. After finding his way back to the main road, he fixed a look of disdain on his face and ignored the curious glances he drew from passers-by as he flip-flopped along, heading in the direction of the ferry port.

Chapter 26

Kennedy and I were friends, rivals, and colleagues: not necessarily in that order. Boyle had manipulated things so that it looked like poor Kennedy was behind a lot of the crime he was trying to solve himself. I was fooled, and I know Theresa was too. He created tensions between us and then exploited them. Meanwhile, Kennedy didn't feel able to confide in anyone. It was really sad. And do I feel guilty?

Every day I sit in his office.

DCI John Tanner

'The passport belongs to the man I'm looking for, but this is not him.' What was it the German woman told him when she translated the book? Trained in espionage and counter- insurgency ... *He has another passport!*

'But that means—' Sayeed didn't get the chance to finish.

'I need to get to the terminal,' Mohand barked, 'and quickly!'

Sayeed flicked his shoulder. 'What are you waiting for? My car is round the corner. Let's go!' He then gave orders to the fresh police arrivals. 'Get those people back. This is a crime scene!'

Pushing through the crowd, Mohand and Sayeed passed another two gendarmes and the ambulance crew coming the other way. 'Don't disturb the body,' Sayeed said, glancing at his watch. 'There's nothing you can do, believe me. Call forensics. I'll be back in a few minutes.'

Although it wasn't a technique he'd employed often, he'd learned years before how to stand out by attracting attention, and yet remain invisible because of it.

Apart from a few cursory glances, people in the queue shunned him, turning to look the other way, purposefully avoiding his brazen gaze. *Shit or bust.*

He handed his passport to the officer in the booth, who looked up and checked the photograph matched the individual. Maintaining a calm and professional air, he double-checked and stared with lingering scrutiny at the parody of a woman before him; he broke contact immediately as the grotesque lips puckered up and blew him a kiss. Stamping the document and handing it back, he jerked his head, indicating he should go through.

Boyle made his way into the heart of the ferry, unsure whether or not his quarry would have taken this particular boat, or tried to shake him off by catching a later one. It didn't matter. All thoughts of kidnapping had disappeared. He despised her with a vengeance and he'd kill her at the first opportunity. *You can run, bitch, but I'll getcha in the end.*

The police had set up a wandering contingent the other side of customs and x-ray to minimize disruption to the queuing. Here people would be stuck for hours anyway.

Miller could see at least two officers making their way between the waiting vehicles. They ordered a woman out of the car. She had a similar hairstyle to Carla.

'Get in the boot,' he urged.

'What's happening?' she said, reacting to his urgent tones.

'Just do it. They've pulled a woman out of a Mercedes up ahead. Now do it quickly!'

'Someone will see me getting in, won't they?' she said, a note of concern in her voice.

'Not if you fold the back seat down, and get into it from there.'

'Jesus, Miller,' she said ruefully, looking down at her new clothes, 'I hope it's clean in there.'

She clambered between the front seats into the back, and lifted the button to let the seat next to her down.

'Go in feet first. That way you can pull it shut after you.'

After a few minutes of close questioning and examination of her passport, the woman was allowed back into her seat.

The officers conversed briefly and then split up.

Miller pushed his sunglasses higher onto the bridge of his nose, cursing himself the instant he did it.

The gendarme's eye was drawn to him and he made a tight circling gesture with his right hand, indicating Miller should open his window.

'Passport, *Monsieur*?'

Miller handed it over.

'Your sunglasses, *Monsieur*,' he said. 'Take them off.'

Miller obliged.

'You have been here for only two days, you no like our country?' Although the officer was smiling, there was a slant of suspicion in his voice. His eyes scanned the inside of the car.

'I'm meeting friends in Spain, and then we're all coming back. In the car.'

'Quicker to fly ...' the gendarme ventured.

'Me, I hate the flying. If I can drive, always I drive.' Miller grinned easily, amused at how his style of speech mirrored that of the other man.

The officer stooped lower, scrutinizing Miller's face. 'The trunk. Open it.'

He thinks I'm a drugs mule! For an instant, he saw how the policeman was viewing him and he knew he'd not given anything away. He smiled again, feeling around under the seat. 'Of course. Do you know where the control is for opening it?'

'Get out of the car, *Monsieur*.'

In his mind, Miller played out the scenario to follow. The officer would crouch down for the release button. All the other policemen were distracted by their own tasks. He would chop him just behind the ear ... *And then what? Are you crazy? Just tell him what happened.*

A voice cried out, '*Arrêter cet homme!* Stop that man!'

The gendarme swivelled around in the direction of the voice. Almost as one, the officers abandoned their previous duties and immediately took up the pursuit.

The running man was built like a rugby prop forward, and was just as evasive.

Miller sighed with relief as whistles blew and all hell broke loose as more people joined the chase.

He relaxed back into his seat. Carla did not say a word, but he imagined her in the boot, seething at hearing the commotion and not knowing what was going on.

A crew member beckoned him forward. He restarted the engine and drove into the bowels of the ship.

Up on the top deck, unnoticed, a tall, dark-skinned ladyboy casually watched the proceedings. The wind played havoc with his long hair and buffeted his loose-fitting traditional clothes. Impassive, he shifted against the railing to face the other way and, hoisting his beach bag over a shoulder, made his way back inside.

Chapter 27

Sayeed stopped the car in the terminal car park.

'Mustafa, you understand you are on your own from here?'

'Sayeed, I'm grateful for your help.'

'What will you do?'

'I will wait here and observe,' he said, pressing his thumb into his navel. 'I have this feeling, here. He will come.'

Catching a glimpse of the commotion ahead, Mohand leaped from the car, thinking it was Boule running and then, realizing it wasn't, called out to the nearest officer, 'You, why are you all chasing that man?'

'He is a suspect in the murder of a German tourist and wanted—'

'It is not him.'

'Then why does he run?'

'Catch him and you will find out, but he is not the man you are supposed to be looking out for. How long has this debacle been going on for?'

The gendarme shrugged. 'Five minutes ...' he said, almost embarrassed.

In one hand, Mohand held his identification aloft and with the other, drew his pistol and fired into the air. The man stopped in his tracks.

A dozen pistols pointed at Mohand. Sayeed stood up, halfway out of the car, leaning on his open door, urging them all to put their guns away. 'He is one of us! Now arrest that man, before someone gets hurt. *Merde*!' Turning to Mohand, he said, 'You had better keep a low profile after that. If the boss hears, he will—'

'Leave him to me. I'm only doing what any off-duty policeman would do. Go, Sayeed. Leave me.'

Miller was one of the last to park. Before leaving the vehicle deck, he opened the back door of the car, and pretended he was looking for something, and then unlatched the back seat, pulling it forward just enough so that he could see Carla's face in the V-shaped aperture. 'It's only for an hour,' he told her; 'you'll just have to endure it.'

'Only an hour! Jeez, what if I need to pee?' she said.

He laughed. 'Put some of that muscle control you've got down there to good use! You've got food and water from that last garage in there with you. Just go easy on the water ...'

'I hate you!' she hissed, as he pushed the back of the seat up, not quite closing it.

'I've left it so you can get out if you absolutely have to, but if you do, be careful. OK?'

As Miller stepped out onto the top deck, a crisp breeze snatched at his clothes. He took a deep breath, and walked into the wind towards the front of the boat.

A saltwater tang in the air, tainted by diesel fumes, gave way to a heady cocktail of memories that washed unexpectedly over him as he leaned, elbows resting on the railings, to look down over the side at the turbulent trail of foam the vessel left in its wake.

He hadn't been on a ferry since Josie died. The churning of the boat as it chugged through the choppy water, and the deep hum of the engines, set off vibrations that combined with his thoughts and started a nausea in his belly. Soon, the sickness would be clawing at the back of his throat.

He looked at his watch. An hour to go. He wasn't sure he'd make it. *Got to stop thinking about it. Got to stop thinking about everything.* But it was too late. Overhead a seabird cried. He saw himself on deck, telescoping out until he was but a speck. He felt his knees give way as if disconnected from his senses, and fought to remain upright. *Mushin no shin.* Mind of no mind. He drifted, and thought once more of Josie; the scene he'd witnessed through the Sister played out in a loop in his head and then stopped. *Stella?*

Although they hadn't spoken, Stella knew Miller was OK. She felt it in the air, in the atmosphere. She'd learned to surrender her thoughts to the void, and have faith in what came back. *Nothing ... If something was wrong, wouldn't I feel it?* She hesitated; something *had* come back. *This is the last time.*

She knew she had to do what she had to do. There'd be no end to it otherwise.

Wandering through the house to Miller's study, she sat down in his chair and opened his notepad. Picking up a pen, she began to write, pausing often, eventually ripping the sheet from the pad and crumpling it into a ball. It was a process she repeated several times as she sought the right words.

She finished writing, folded the note, and placed it in front of her on his desk, on top of the accumulation of letters that also awaited his return.

She pushed herself away to gather the rejected balls of paper. About to throw them in the wastepaper bin, she noticed a similarly crumpled ball resting at the bottom.

She frowned, wondering if she'd thrown one in separately from the others without thinking. She took it out and studied it. The compression was far tighter than those she had in her other hand. She unwrapped it and smoothed the creases from the page, and Miller's handwriting was revealed.

Dear Stella,

I wanted to explain something before I left because you were in no mood to listen to me. When I get back, I'll go through it all then – why I had to finish this thing once and for all.

This will be the last time. I promise.

Bruce x

She sat down again, thinking about what he'd said. Why didn't he give her the message? Why did he throw it away? Slowly shaking her head, she remembered that he'd said it would be the last time when he'd gone off with Carla to Amsterdam. No, she was right. It would never be over. It suddenly occurred to her that she hadn't said goodbye. She analysed her thoughts. *It isn't really goodbye, is it? You're going to see him again. It's just a warning shot, to give him a scare. You wouldn't leave him. How could you?*

She smiled, recalling how she'd caught him with his beloved seashell at his ear; after such a long separation from it, he was again listening to the whispers it breathed from its mysterious and labyrinthine interior.

'It's a return to childhood memories and comforts ...,' he'd said.

'I don't know how you can so fondly stroke that thing, when the last person who held it died in such tragic circumstances.'

He'd looked at her at length. 'You don't get it, do you? For a long time I thought when I threw it to Brooks, as he was drowning, that its magic had failed ... I did tell you how I acquired it in the first place, didn't I?'

'You did.'

'Well, when I got it back, at the hospital, it started me thinking that it hadn't failed at all. My strong association with it kept Brooks and the other boys alive in my memory, frozen in time, just as they were that day ...' He'd trailed off, allowing his thoughts to catch up.

She'd seen it in the deepening lines of his face as his eyes narrowed, focusing on a point beyond where she was sitting, somewhere distant in his mind.

'I learned a lot from that experience, but you know what came to me in a flash?'

She shook her head. He clearly hadn't told her everything.

'No one ever really dies. We carry a tiny part of them around in here.' He tapped his temple. 'In our memories. The more important the person is to us ... the more loved they were, then the stronger this little thing is.' He glanced at her. 'You're not following me, are you?' He pushed his hands together so that the tips of his fingers and thumbs touched, prayer-like. 'This is what I think. This little thing, a memory pocket if you like, is always at some point in our minds, depending on where we want it to be, but it's always there. And someone doesn't have to be dead for it to work. I've said this so often. How many times have you thought about a friend you haven't seen for years, and then the telephone rings – and it's them. Or, walking down the high street, you think of a particular person and then turn a corner and bump into them. It happens more often than for mere chance to be at play. The memory pocket is, I believe, both a transmitter and a receiver. Most people have forgotten how to use it. It's a throwback to our

132

ancestors, to before we communicated with the spoken word. Now we only see it at work rarely, in the quiet moments, when our thinking is abstract, or something. We tap into a sort of cosmic consciousness and through those memories we send a signal and, sometimes, it's received.'

'You started out by saying no one ever really dies as long as we remember them ...'

'That's right. I also came round to thinking it helps explain why some people say they smelled their mother's perfume years after she'd died, and felt her presence. The memory pocket came alive and brought her back, just for a few moments, and it works when we most need comfort from despair, or something like that.'

She remembered how it made perfect sense. For her, when Boyle had her in his clutches, it was her father she'd recalled, and she'd gained solace from his memory.

'And the seashell?' she'd asked.

'It had something ... I don't know how, but it gave Brooks enough tangibility to give it back when I really needed it.' He'd turned the shell over, wrapped it in a soft black cloth and put it in the top drawer next to where she now sat. 'I don't need it for my memories. I never did. I hope I never need it for anything else.'

Her fingers found the handle of the drawer, and she opened it. The shell had gone.

Chapter 28

Lieutenant Mohand knew he couldn't delay the sailing; he had no jurisdiction. If he wanted to test his hunch, he had no choice other than to go aboard and make the crossing. If Boule wasn't on the boat, it meant one of two things: he'd either gone and Mohand wouldn't have to concern himself any further, or he was still in Morocco.

His instincts told him that in the light of the most recent developments, he would be on the ship.

He flashed his ID card and boarded the ferry.

Passengers swarmed in all directions, heading up the stairways that led to the upper decks. He stood to one side. *Where would they most likely be?* To cover the whole thing on his own was like sweeping for fish with a tiny net on the end of a bamboo cane. If he started at the top and worked his way down, he reasoned, he might have a better chance. The futility of the exercise dawned on him and, at almost the same time, a possible solution to the immediate problem came to mind.

Get ashore first and pick them out of the crowd coming off the boat.

If they were on board, that's how he'd do it. But if they *were* on there, how had they managed it without being detected?

He turned various scenarios over in his mind. Boule, instantly recognizable, must have smuggled himself on, concealed in a car or lorry.

He made his way down to the vehicle hold.

As soon as the boat had chugged clear of port, it surged to full speed. On the upper deck, Miller steadied himself, chin on chest, and leaning partly over the top rail he gripped it in each hand, holding on. With knees slightly bent, and one foot behind the other, he looked as if he were stretching, about to commence exercise.

He measured his breathing, counting one-two-three on each rise, and then did the same on each fall of his chest. Swallowing saliva with increased frequency, he bowed at the railing, still trying to hold back the inevitable. His phone buzzed in his pocket. He ignored it. Rapid chimes indicated a cluster of received messages. *What the ...? It's working again! Stella...? It has to be her.*

He straightened, removed one hand from the railing and dug deep into his pocket with it to retrieve his mobile.

Nine new messages. All from Stella.

He swayed unsteadily as he released the rail with his other hand, and with feet planted wide, scrolled back to read the first of them.

The phone rang. He almost dropped it.

'Stella,' he said, taking a deep breath, 'where the hell have you been?'

'Bruce, I can't do this anymore ...'

'Wha—'

'No, don't interrupt. I've been worried *sick*. You don't answer your phone, you don't answer my texts. Leaving cryptic messages for me to find at home just doesn't cut it with me anymore.' She ran out of breath.

He jumped in. 'Hey, that's not my fault! There's been a problem with the signal, the network or something. I've tried calling and texting loads of times,' he said, adding quickly, 'Anyway, I'm on my way home now.'

'With her?' she said, with undisguised venom.

'Not, *with* her – not in the way you just said – but she's here. In the boot of the car, as a matter of fact.'

Silence.

'Stella?'

'I'm here, I'm just thinking. What on earth is she doing in the boot of your car? What car? I'm almost afraid to ask what's going on but, you see, that's what I'm talking about.'

What's that in her voice? Resignation: but to what? 'Are you thinking about leaving me?' he said.

'When you took off with her, *you* left *me*. You've been gone ... what is it, three, four days? I can't even think ... *you* left me. I've had enough in my life of being left. I thought you'd be different.'

'Look, about that photograph—' he began.

'It isn't about the photograph! I'm not so stupid I don't know what she's trying to pull ...' She stopped suddenly, thinking about her new tattoo and how she'd reconciled herself to competing with her, how she had believed what he said was true and what she'd felt when she'd opened that book. No more.

Something had changed. She felt uneasy. The line went dead. A feeling of dread seized her. Frantically, she pressed the redial button. She hadn't finished talking. She'd wanted to say, 'We'll talk when you get home.'

There was no answer. 'Oh, God!' she cried, tilting her face heavenward. 'One more chance, but it's the last time.' The feeling in the pit of her stomach wouldn't go away. 'We didn't say goodbye,' she whispered.

'Stella, are you there?' he said, sensing she'd gone.

He stood with his face to the wind; vaporized mists of seawater sprinkled his face. Raising his voice, he repeated her name. 'Stella?'

With his back to the rest of the deck, focusing on her, he sensed something not right.

A female voice, immediately behind, wheedled, mocking him. 'Stella, are you there, Stella?'

He froze. It sounded like Stella, but it couldn't be. He'd just been talking with her; she was in England.

He didn't need to spin around to see who it was.

The sickness he'd been keeping at bay seeped into his gullet. Slowly, he turned to face the monster who stood behind him.

'You!' Boyle said, pointing his finger. 'I should have known you had something to do with all this.'

Miller stared directly into the face of the evil he'd first encountered as a child, and shuddered at the mask he wore: rouged, ladyboy lips, high cheekbones, flesh pulled impossibly tight, emphasizing his broken nose, white where the skin stretched over the bridge of it.

Miller's eyes finally settled on the fist his enemy had made.

He read the word the letters of each tattooed knuckle formed. *Wrath.*

'You know what happens now, don't you?' Boyle said, closing the gap between them.

Chapter 29

'You got lucky before, but this time I'm ready for you, sonny boy. This is going to sting a bit.'

Miller looked into his adversary's face.

Boyle glared back, his eyes flickering as he watched Miller's lower body for sudden leg movement.

He thinks I'm going to try to sweep him, and he's on guard against it. Miller feinted with a left jab, dropped down and tried the sweep, thinking to double-bluff the old fighter.

Boyle skipped over his leading leg and then, before Miller could regain his footing, closed him off into the corner of the barrier behind.

Miller cursed his stupidity. A shotgun charge of adrenalin fired through his veins. His heart galloped a double pump. A long-forgotten dream returned. Kirk, his former mentor and teacher, demonstrated a series of moves. It had worked before. He had to act without thinking. *Mushin.* Mind of no mind. Empty mind.

Boyle reached for him. He felt the press of the warm steel rail against his back and, quick as a flash, he catapulted, folding forward at the waist.

Boyle moved swiftly to counter, but he reacted to the move he thought Miller was making, and not to the one he actually made.

Using his forward momentum, Miller ducked beneath Boyle's arm and spun on the axis of the foot remaining on the deck, while the other foot whipped round high and struck Boyle hard on the chin.

Boyle wobbled, a look of incredulity on his face, cursing his underestimation of the younger man.

Miller kicked the back of his enemy's knee, the one bearing most weight, hard.

Boyle twisted away and steadied himself against the railing, lashing out with a donkey kick, catching Miller in the stomach.

Air exploded from Miller's abdomen, and he sagged to his knees.

'Got you, boy! The strongest wins at last.'

Grabbing him by the arm, he swung Miller hard against the railings. One hand clamped around his throat, he forced his head backwards, while the other hand kept his right arm pinned down.

From the position he was in, Miller couldn't fight back with efficacy, but still he tried.

The crushing, brute strength of the older man proved too much for him; the old fighter, too wily to give up his advantage, forced him over the railings.

He's going to squeeze the last drop of life from me, and throw me in. He'd lost touch with his inner self, couldn't connect. *Mushin.* Too late, he realized it was some kind of summoning. All strength had deserted him. He looked down and saw the water below. *Come by water.* He couldn't feel his legs. He fixed Boyle with a last look. The shark-like eyes stared coldly back at him. A passing regret at leaving Carla in the boot of the car turned into full-blown grief at the realization he'd never see Stella again.

Carla's enforced isolation grated on her nerves. She'd endured her cramped position in the boot of the car for long enough. She'd get out, stretch her legs, find Miller, have a drink with him and be back in place ten minutes before the ferry docked, easily. She pushed the seat forward and, using the back of the front seat to hold onto, wriggled out, and up against the vertical surface, like a cobra about to strike. Vertebrae creaked at the base of her spine as she completed the manoeuvre. She reached back in, and pulled out the two one-litre bottles of Pepsi she'd purchased on their last pit stop.

After checking to see if the coast was clear, she opened the back door and climbed out.

At the far end of the deck, over the sound of the engines, Mohand heard the boom of a car door closing. He scanned the area quickly, looking for signs of movement. A steel door opened. He switched focus and for the briefest instant before it closed again, he caught a glimpse of a dark-haired woman. His heart beating faster, he dashed, zig-zagging between the parked cars until he reached the same door and, pulling on it, listened for the sound of footsteps on the metal stairs. The noise cascading from above cloaked everything else. He looked at his watch. *Forty minutes before the ship docks.*

He began his ascent.

Carla knew where he'd be. When she'd first met Miller, it was on a long train journey and after some initial reticence, he'd opened up and told her some things. He only ever used air travel as a last resort, and *boats* ... she grinned. Well, he hated the water, so it was obvious he didn't like sea travel either. She trudged the last few steps with aching thighs; the bottles she carried weighed her down further. She'd thought she'd met her Mr Right. The stories he'd led her to had ended up pulling them apart. She wondered if it hadn't been for his meeting Stella, would they have had a chance?

Stepping through the doorway onto the upper deck, she noticed nearly everyone looking on at a fight taking place up against the railings at the bow end of the boat. It took a moment to register. *Miller?* He seemed to be struggling with a large, long-haired, sarong-clad woman.

She's too big to be female ...

The realization spurred her on. She broke into a run, and then sprinted towards them. One of the bottles fell from her arms, half-bouncing, half-rolling as it lost momentum behind her.

Miller's desperately grasping hand found a loose end of Boyle's sarong. Holding it firmly, he stared in defiance, and wound it around his wrist. If he went, Boyle was going with him.

Crump! Boyle's eyes flashed wide, shocked at the lightning bolt of pain that ripped through his head as shards of bone from his unhealed skull fracture pierced his brain.

Crump! An explosion of fizzing black liquid showered Miller and dripped from the ends of Boyle's long dark wig.

Thwack! The cracked, broken plastic sound of the now empty bottle of Pepsi being wielded by Carla was the last thing he heard.

Boyle staggered, desperately clinging to life. With eyesight failing, to prevent himself falling – or perhaps, in his final moments, before his senses failed, determined to take Miller with him – he grabbed the crook of the younger man's elbow and locked on.

Caught off balance, Miller tried to jerk his arm free, but the killer's grip, like the teeth of a savage terrier, held firm.

Carla watched horrified as the two men went over the rails together. She fell to her knees.

In the fleeting seconds that followed, she noticed things. Miller's phone lay face up on the deck, spinning in a lazy circle, driven by the vibration of the incoming call. Stella's happy face illuminated the screen. Crazily, she thought about picking it up. She was aware of people, a dozen or more. Not one had intervened but, now the fight had finished, the ones who weren't huddling up to their children sprang to life, rushing towards the handrail where the two men had gone over.

Then the screaming began.

A swarthy Saddam Hussein lookalike skidded into view, looking left and then right. They locked eyes.

'Carla Black?' he yelled. 'Police! I want to talk to you!'

'Man overboard!' she shouted and, vaulting the rails, plunged over the side.

Chapter 30

Unwitnessed, moments earlier, a bizarre, twirling pirouette display happened in mid-air during the seconds it took for the two men to fall sixty feet.

Miller struck the water first.

Boyle smacked down on top of him.

The double impact drove the air from Miller's lungs. Reflex sucked seawater in to replace it. *Water...*

He was driven ten feet beneath the surface before the initial velocity was countered by the sea. Although he'd never learned to swim, his legs scissored in a subconscious reaction to his predicament.

Darkness bore down on him. A deadweight.

He choked, tried to control it, but each stifled cough leaked precious air and took in more liquid.

Mushin. What good is there in thinking that now? You're gone, boy. He looked up. Boyle was on top of him, forcing him down. Revulsion at the thought of ending up on the seabed in that position spurred him into action, and he pushed himself clear.

Above, way beyond his reach, he fixed his eyes on the surface. *This is it. Me and you kid, returned to the sea.*

He fished the shell from his pocket and held it.

Whispered promises made came back to him. Too late for those things now.

The light above was replaced by darkness.

If she'd been able to check, Carla would have discovered that only ten seconds had passed between the men going over the side and her following.

She hit the water like a ball, with her head, legs and arms tucked in tight, unfurling them as she went under.

Knowing the vessel had covered perhaps a hundred metres in the intervening moments, she started to swim in the right direction before even reaching the surface.

A marker buoy splashed into the sea behind her. *Not even close.*

She swam hard, at first following the length of the ship. Her eyes locked onto a point on the horizon; she realized the ferry was moving away from her.

It was turning.

For what seemed an eternity she drove herself through the water. *Where are you?*

A floating mass of hair caught between her fingers.

She recoiled, and shook it free.

The realization of what it was, and what it meant, hit her.

She realized the tangled mess of wig hair belonged to Boyle and then, peering into the depths below, she saw Miller's white upturned face at the edge of the shimmering limits of light penetration.

She gulped a lungful of air and dived beneath the choppy surface.

How long had he been like this? She took his head and, pressing her lips over his, breathed air into him while kicking for the surface. She'd underestimated her own needs. On her own she might have made it, but two of them? No chance. If she released him and went for another breath, he'd sink again. They'd be back to square one.

The sun's shifting, marbling effect made it hard for her to judge. *Ten feet? It may as well be fifty.*

She relaxed her muscles and let his body go.

He slid through her grip, sinking, his outstretched right arm scraping down her body. She couldn't look at him. His head brushed into her legs, going down. She lingered. *This isn't how my story is supposed to end. Without him, what would I be?* At the last possible moment, just at the limit of her reach, she caught him. His fingers were held fast around an object. She probed with her fingertips to try to hold his hand; pushing them into his fist, she felt a smooth hard surface. *I can't hold on.*

Neither could she let go.

The muffled sound of a fast-approaching engine resonated under the water.

Twenty minutes later, the fast border control boat docked. A waiting ambulance took two prone bodies from the boat.

Chapter 31

21 November 2007

The sky outside darkened, causing the interior of the spare room Carla had designated as her office, to grow dim. She squinted at the screen. *Too bright*. She rose from her chair, reached for the table lamp and switched it on, reducing the glare.

She resumed typing the last of the additional chapters she'd added to her book. The final one had given her more trouble than all the others put together. Rereading what she'd written for the umpteenth time, she was aware of a draught that had blown in from somewhere, and then a few spots of rain hit the windows and dribbled down the glass. For a time, she stopped what she was doing and just stared at the words on the screen.

Who'd have thought you could kill a man with a bottle of Pepsi? It seems likely that an earlier, unhealed skull injury collapsed under the impact as I struck him, causing fatal brain damage. Miller said he saw the light go out of his eyes at the very first blow. I hit him twice, as hard as I could, before the bottle exploded on the third whack.

When they went over the side, I knew I had to act quickly. With the boat travelling at around twenty to twenty-five knots, it was covering ten metres with each passing second. I also knew that if the fall hadn't killed him, he couldn't swim – and on top of that, I didn't know Boyle was dead.

I couldn't believe how high up we were: sixty feet I was told later. If I hadn't leaped without thinking, I might not have done it, and this book would have had a rather different, tragic ending ...

I still can't remember a thing after I'd given Miller my last breath.

I must have simply passed out from exhaustion. All those evenings spent in the swimming pool paid off in ways I could never have imagined. It's hard to believe the crew hoisted us on board on the end of a huge pole, but that's what Lieutenant Mohand told me. He was grateful for my help in clearing up a few matters pertaining to Boule, as he called him. I couldn't get used to his old Foreign Legion name; he was Boyle to me.

I couldn't tell Mohand the whole story. Uncertain if I'd broken some law, how could I?

Still not right. It doesn't seem complete. She saved her work and resolved to come back to it later.

A walk in the rain; that's what she needed. No better way to clear her head. A thought struck her. She'd call the revised edition *The Life and Times of William Boule.*

Opening a drawer in the desk beside her, she removed the sketch her friend Chloe, a seasoned police artist, had drawn, and smoothed the crinkles from it as best she could. It still amazed her how she'd created such an incredible likeness from words alone. She smiled as she remembered how she'd snatched it from Chloe's grasp in her haste to get going, causing her thumb to smudge the left-hand edge, and Chloe crying out after her, 'But I haven't finished!'

The room illuminated in a burst of sunlight.

She pushed the chair back and walked to the window. Outside, jewelled drops of rain on the grass refracted light, creating myriads of tiny rainbows. Raising her eyes, she marvelled at the multicoloured arch that spanned the sky. She would keep the artist's impression on the cover of the revised edition. *She'd like that,* she thought fondly.

Stella passed the book back to Miller. 'I read the original while you were in Morocco. Is that really what she did, plan the whole thing just so she could finish the story on a high note?'

'She'd do anything for a story.'

'She nearly got you killed. That poor little Arab boy ...' she said, shaking her head.

'I know, but I went into it with my eyes open. I went there in the hope I'd get the chance to finish Boyle one way or another. I think you can understand now why I couldn't tell you, why I had to leave you behind.'

She nodded. 'Do you think he'd have got her?'

'No doubt about that.'

'What about him? It says in the book the authorities never recovered the body.'

'A week after it was published, they found a body washed up on shore. At first they thought it was an illegal immigrant who'd drowned attempting the crossing to Spain – they get a lot of them falling off boats; some of them even try swimming it. Anyway, the face was half-chewed off and they identified him initially from the tattoo that spelled 'wrath' on his hand. They're comparing the DNA with blood samples they took after Eilise Stapleton bashed him with a rounders bat. But it's him.'

'How can you be so sure ahead of the DNA results?'

'I think he died as soon as Carla hit him, more or less straightaway. He was dead when he hit the water, and if he wasn't, he definitely drowned.'

'It's kind of ironic, isn't it? That he should be killed at sea on a ferry ... like karma for what he did to Josie. She disappeared while on a ferry, didn't you say?'

His eyebrows gathered. 'Yes ...' In his mind's eye he flashed back to the vision the Sister had shared with him: a maelstrom of complex feelings tore through him, overwhelming him. Struggling to pick them apart, he saw Josie on a ship's deck, alone at the rail. Boyle approached from behind and savagely attacked her ... when it was over, he'd heaved her overboard, into the sea. 'It was weird this time. I never had the near-death experiences I'd had before and, yet, I've been thinking about it ... The whole thing ... every part of it was preordained ... jigsaw pieces, cut and neatly fitted into place. If they'd been squares or circles, I'd have seen it sooner, but then ... even that was part of the plan.'

She smiled. 'You know something?'

'What?'

'You think about things too much.'

'Maybe ... By the way, did I tell you she's signed an exclusive serialization deal with a national newspaper?'

She shook her head. 'No, you didn't.' The lines in her forehead deepened. 'Can you hate someone and admire them at the same time?'

'Is that how you feel about Carla?'

'Yes, it is. How do you feel about her?'

He didn't answer straightaway. 'She saved my life—'

'She nearly got you killed.'

'I know, but I'm still here, and Boyle isn't.' Seeing she was about to say something, he raised a hand. 'No, let me finish. She's got her faults, no doubt about that, but she does have some good points—'

'Hah! Like what ...?' She grimaced. 'No, don't tell me.'

'Nothing like that, not like you,' he said, and smiled. 'She's selfish, that's true, but underneath it all, she's got a good heart.'

'A good heart?' She guffawed. 'Are you kidding me? What about that photograph ...?'

He'd known this moment was coming. 'Yes ... I should never have trusted her with my phone ...' He met her gaze. 'Why are you grinning at me like that?'

She switched on her phone and handed it to him.

His eyes widened. 'Is this you? Holy shit ...' He turned the image around in his hand against the light.

'Want a better look?' she said and, pulling him up, led him by the hand to the bedroom.

Afterwards, spent of all energy, Miller closed his eyes. Stella grinned and nudged him. 'I haven't finished with you yet ...'

He rolled from his back to face her.

'She's one of those people that can't just do something on their own, isn't she? She has to drag everyone else in, but especially you.'

'It's twice,' he said. 'That was the second time.'

'Well, it's once too often. I should be asking you to promise you won't go off at her beck and call again, but I won't. A promise is a powerful thing. What I will do, though, is promise you something. If it happens again for no good reason, like saving the world or something, then I'll go, because I couldn't ...' She bit into her lower lip.

'I know,' he said, and moved closer, feeling her warm skin against his.

'I'm going to ask you to do something else, though.'

'What's that?'

'Stay away from anywhere you can drown. By the way, while you were gone I noticed you'd taken your shell out of the drawer.'

'And?'

'I was a lot happier when it was in there.'

He retrieved his jeans from the floor and took it from his pocket, handing it to her. 'I told you about this, didn't I? There isn't another one like it in the entire world.'

'It's that special, is it? Or do you mean it's like a fingerprint?' The hand she held it in bobbed up and down as she felt the weight of it. 'It's warm,' she said.

'It's been in my pocket ...'

'But you took your trousers off ages ago ...' She held it to her ear. Her eyes lit up. 'I can hear the sea,' she said.

She'd taken a gamble, very nearly lost her life, but been instrumental in ridding the world of a monster who'd evaded detection for forty years. Carla thought back to the dinner date she'd had with David Mailer at the beginning, and how it had borne fruit.

She'd known David had fancied her from their time working together at the *News of The World*. He didn't need much convincing. The tryst after dinner, the details of her proposal finalized ... Although she'd arrived back in England before the deadline agreed with all parties, she'd kept quiet, allowing the wheels of fate to turn in her favour. She smiled as she recollected how she'd not actually slept with him.

It had been a very rewarding blow job.

Following the serialization of her book, she'd released it in all formats. The story she'd seen when she'd first met Miller had borne more fruit than she'd ever imagined. She'd written a bestseller. The exclusive fee from the newspaper had been unprecedented for an unknown author. The dedication read simply: *For my father, Henry, war correspondent.*

Chapter 32

The date on Miller's newspaper drew his eye: 27 November …
Even after all these years, he remembered: it was Josie's birthday.
He lost himself, staring at the front page without reading anything.

A momentary blare of sound from outside, accompanied by a
drop in temperature, distracted him from his emerging memories.

He looked up with curiosity. The staff gathered at the service
end of the counter turned as one to greet someone who had entered
the French cafe, causing a flurry of activity among the young male
waiters. He couldn't see, from where he was sitting, who it was.

Returning to the paper, he caught a whiff of familiar perfume.
His olfactory memory confirmed it only a second before she
appeared.

'I knew I'd find you in here,' Carla said, unhitching her jacket
from her shoulders. 'You don't mind, do you?'

He shrugged and indicated the table place opposite. 'Stella
would go ape, if she knew.'

She hung her jacket over the back of the chair and sat down.
'Are you going to tell her?'

'Well, I just bumped into you. What's to hide?'

None of the cutlery had been used; black coffee steamed in the
cup in front of him. 'Not having breakfast?' she said, licking her
lips.

'If it's on you, then maybe … I'm glad to see you, actually.'

'You are?'

'Yes, I am,' he said, a smile ghosting his lips. 'You owe me for
that iPhone and the clothes—'

'Hang on,' she retorted, 'I ruined everything saving your life, remember?'

'I'd have put it down as a business expense,' he countered, 'but it wasn't my business to book it to, or claim against ...' He sipped his coffee.

'You know what, Miller? You've turned into a real tightwad.'

He fought to keep the hot liquid from spewing out of his mouth, almost choking in the process. Dabbing at his lips with a napkin, he raised an eyebrow and said one word: '*Me?*'

'I'm not tight,' she said, adding with a wicked smile, 'Not in that sense anyway, as you well know.'

'Carla – why are you here?'

'I don't know how to ask, really,' she said, 'but I need another story—'

Miller shook his head slowly. 'Carla, I can't help you.'

'I'm not asking you to get involved, just to give me another one to write – we'll split the proceeds.'

'That's generous, but I've got nothing for you ...'

'Then I'll have no choice but to resurrect the Donovan Kale case ...'

Miller stared at her. Would she do it? 'I'll think about it,' he lied. 'Speaking of splitting the proceeds, how about donating my share of *The Life and Times* to charity?'

Her eyes shifted under his steady gaze. 'We never agreed to anything like that, and besides,' she said, 'I didn't do as well with selling the story as I'd hoped.' Something in her face changed, as she added, 'Your saying that reminds me ...'

Registering the look of faraway sadness, he asked, 'Of what?'

'I've got to go back there ... to honour a promise I made to Mohammed: that I'd give his family some money ...'

He nodded in quiet acquiescence.

'The thing is ... how do I find out where they live now? It was like a rabbit warren, and I only went there the once ... I don't want to go through Mohand, just in case something's turned up since we left, and I get arrested.'

'Like what?' he said. 'You did tell me everything, didn't you?'

'I think so but, you know, it's a foreign country ... I was reading about a case there involving police taking females as sex slaves.'

'The police did that?'

'I'm telling you ...'

'That would make quite a story,' he ventured, beaming with mirth.

Carla narrowed her eyes, but they gleamed with humour. 'I only go so far for a story,' she said. 'Now, getting back to where we were. How would you find them?'

Miller pressed his lips tight with concentration. 'I'm not so sure I can help much. I used to be more in touch with things, but the intuitions I once had just come and go now. I think I'm only set to one station. It's weird.'

'I only asked if you could help. If you can't, you can't,' she said, shrugging. 'What do you mean, only tuned to one station?'

'I was thinking about this only the other day ...' he said. 'How best to explain it to you?' He scratched an eyebrow. 'Imagine you're in a car and the radio is an old model. You get the signal only as long as the car is in range. Beyond that, all you get is static.'

'You need a new radio,' she said, raising her eyebrows. 'Or learn to fix the old one. Anyway, what would you do to find out where his family live?'

He looked around the cafe and, satisfied no one could see, took her hand and closed his eyes.

His hand felt warm in hers, the tips of his fingers warmer still. Did she imagine a tingling sensation? She couldn't be sure.

Releasing his grip, he shook his head and said, 'Nothing, sorry. It's all down to you ...'

Later that night, as sleep beckoned her from consciousness, she thought about Miller. She'd kept a diary on him dating back to their first encounter on the train. She'd called it *The Miller Stories*, and arranged the records chronologically. *I must take a look through it in the morning.*

On the cusp of losing coherent thought, ideas jockeyed for attention. A lecture Miller had given her on the value of things lingered in her mind. What exactly did he mean? She'd been drunk at the time. Her eyes flew open.

The chase out of town. When Mohammed had scootered her out of danger her brain, alive with adrenaline, had taken in much more than she could recall. In her semi-somnolent state, without distraction of any sort, the journey out to his house played back for her.

Immediately after turning out of the market side street, the boy had turned left. Her hands gripped tight on either side of his slim waist as the machine picked up speed, her torn blouse flapping in the slipstream. *Where had he gone next?*

He'd turned again, past a school. A red-haired woman waved.

'That is my teacher from when I was at this school,' he'd said, full of pride, as he'd raised his hand to return the greeting.

The school: she'd find the school. Speak to the teacher. Find out where the family lived from there. But how would she do it without revealing her part in the boy's demise?

It occurred to her, as she drifted off, that her fingertips were tingling.

Chapter 33

Essaouira, 25 January 2008

Carla watched the children leaving school in the afternoon. She hoped the red-haired teacher still worked there. She hesitated, and changed her mind about going in. It would be easier to approach her in the street.

A stiff breeze ensured it was too cold for standing still, far colder than when she'd last been in town, so she paced up and down the street outside the main entrance gate to keep warm. She checked her watch. She wondered if the teacher may have exited from another gate. It was Friday. If she didn't see her today, she'd have to rethink her plans.

Four o'clock. She'd waited over an hour. Reluctant to leave, she decided to wait another ten minutes. The wind carried the sound of women's laughter from behind, as they left the school grounds. She stopped and turned, waiting for them to come into sight.

They turned out of the gate and onto the pavement, heading away from her. The teacher was with two others. She'd hoped to make the approach on a one-to-one basis. She followed at a distance as the three walked on. *If she gets into a car, I'm screwed.*

The group separated at the first corner. The redhead continued on her own.

Carla upped her pace and caught her.

'*Excusez-moi,*' she said.

The other woman stopped and turned to face her. 'English, I assume?' she said.

'How can you tell?' Carla said, genuinely puzzled.

'Your accent is terrible, a dead giveaway. How can I help?'

'My name's Carla. I want to trace a young boy by the name of Mohammed. He used to come to this school ...'

'I'm Rusty,' she said. 'You'll need to do better than that to find him. Half the kids around here are called Mohammed.'

'Really?'

'Yes. Well, not half, but a lot of them,' she said. 'May I ask what it is you want with the boy?'

'His father is a taxi driver ...'

'That helps, but only a little. You haven't answered my question.'

Carla said, 'I met him once, in town – he was my guide for a couple of days. We got separated before I could pay him. I'm staying in Marrakech. I couldn't be this close and not try to find him.'

'I see,' Rusty said. 'In the summer was it?'

'Yes,' she lied.

'They're all guides in the summer. I can't help you.' Rusty walked on.

'That's such a shame,' Carla called after her. 'He broke my heart with his story about how he was left to look after his brothers and sisters when his mother died ...'

Rusty stopped. 'Come with me. I live two hundred metres from here.'

Once inside the apartment, the teacher said, 'I'll get us something to drink as soon as I've done this.' She hastily put together the makings of a joint. 'Really good stuff, this,' she said as she crumbled the hash onto a bed of tobacco. 'Don't even have to heat it up, not like that dreadful stuff we get back in Europe.' She mixed the two ingredients evenly and then rolled the thin paper into a club-shaped cigarette. Lighting it, she inhaled deeply. She continued speaking while holding her breath; her voice sounded strained.

'Do I remember him? Of course I do. He left school to look after his family when his mother died. Brilliant little footballer. What happened to him was tragic.' She blew a plume of smoke at the ceiling and then continued. 'They had high hopes for him ... they ... I'm sorry,' she said, and wept.

Carla fought back tears, but said nothing.

Rusty took another puff, and held the joint out for Carla.

'I'd better not,' she said. 'I've got to get back to Marrakech tonight, and I'll probably get lost if I smoke any of that stuff.'

The teacher took another puff, and then placed it in the ashtray. 'Phew, that's enough for now. Helps me unwind, you see. But too much and I forget what I'm supposed to be doing. Did I get us that tea?'

Carla put a hand out and said, 'Don't worry ... if you can just give me an address, I'll get out of your hair.'

'That poor family really has gone through it,' Rusty said, staring glassy-eyed at the stream of smoke billowing from the end of the cigarette. 'How much do you owe him? Can't be much. Leave it with me and I'll see it gets to him.'

'His family, you mean?'

'Whatever ... I shouldn't have had that last puff,' she said, a Cheshire cat grin fixed on her face. 'What did you say before that?'

'The address, can you give me the address? I want to take the money in person.'

Rusty looked blank. 'I don't think I know it ... but I know where it is.'

Carla unfolded the Google map she'd printed out. 'Can you show me on there?'

Taking the map, Rusty turned it all the way through 360 degrees. 'Just getting my bearings,' she said. 'Ah, here we are, here.' Holding her thumb over the spot, she reached onto the coffee table and picked up a pen. Marking the spot with an X, she squinted at the outer edge of the page. 'It's somewhere here ... I think you may have cut the edge of the page off showing where you want ... no, wait, here it is, here ... It's the last house down on the left, with a blue door.' She drew a line down through the alleyways leading from the main road. 'There,' she said, checking the route a second time. 'That's as much as I can do. Will you be OK? I'm sorry, I should take you there, but you know how it is ...' She eyed her joint.

'Thanks, Rusty. How long to walk it?'

'Don't walk, get a cab,' she said, closing her eyes.

The driver dropped her right outside. She had to smile. *The last house down, with a blue door.* All the doors were blue. The entrance seemed familiar, though, and the door creaked as she let herself in. Blinking in the reduced light, she moved to the left and knocked at the door of his apartment.

Mohammed's father answered.

A taxi driver by trade, his memory for places and people was excellent. He had a large spoon in his left hand. 'What you want? You have caused this family enough grief.'

'I know, I ... I just wanted—'

'I do not care what you wanted. Go, now.'

'To give you some money, that's what I wanted.' She took the envelope from her bag and held it out to him.

He snatched it from her. 'Money!' he spat in disgust. 'You think the money can change what you did? Get away from my door,' he said, brandishing the spoon.

She staggered back.

He slammed the door.

Well, what else did you really expect, Carla? That he'd say you were forgiven? The lightness of her step had disappeared as she trudged out the way she'd come in, pulling the door closed behind her.

She headed for the top of the alley.

Deep in thought, she'd covered twenty paces before a door rasped on its hinges, opening to her left. An elderly woman dressed in black peered at her through the gap, eyes filled with suspicion. Back down the street, another door creaked as it opened. *Don't they oil the bloody hinges out here?* Absently, she concluded that it must be all that sandy dust.

Something Miller once said came to her, his voice in her head. *If everything's for sale, then what price do you put on soul?* Well, at least he took the money. Maybe it was best that the father had banged the door in her face.

A tap-tapping sound, followed by the rasping scrape of something metallic dragging, filtered into her consciousness, getting faster, building like some crazy jazz rhythm.

She didn't turn around. Instead, she picked up her pace.

'Lady?'

She froze.

'Is that you, lady?'

Her heart leaped. *It can't be.*

She turned slowly, as if in a dream, to face the boy lurching towards her with one leg in calipers, steadying himself with a Zimmer frame.

'Mohammed?'

She ran to him. 'I've never been more pleased to see anyone in my life ... but how?'

The boy's pale face lit up with a smile. 'Allah, he say, I no want you now. Later, maybe. Now, I just take football life … the rest, you keep.'

She wept.

Mohammed shuffled closer and took her hand. 'No cry, lady ... please. My father, he say I am miracle boy – come back from the dead. For this, we celebrate.'

Wiping her face dry, she said, 'Of course, but your leg … it looks so bad.' She nodded towards the scaffold-like apparatus enclosing his broken limb. 'Will you be able to walk properly again, without those things?'

'In one more operation, maybe two, he will be better. But I keep him, lady,' he said, leaning on the Zimmer.

A distant and now familiar creak reached her ears.

'Mohammed,' his father bellowed, '*sortir de cette prostituée.*'

Carla cringed, stung by the words.

'I have to go,' he said, turning away. 'He blames you, lady, for this. But I say, no, this is the will of Allah, who does no thing for no reason.' Completing his manoeuvre, he spoke over his shoulder, '*Au revoir*, lady, fare you well.'

'And you, Mohammed,' she said, tears dripping from her cheeks. 'And you.'

She stood watching him lunge and scrape towards his father, who hissed something unintelligible, gesturing for the boy to hurry.

At the door, Mohammed slowly turned, completing the process of changing direction, and lifted the frame through the opening.

She had her hand half-raised, ready to wave.

He went inside without looking back.

In the morning Carla got up early and made a few telephone calls, one of them to a friend who worked in the claims department of a medical insurance company.

'Jilly, it's Carla ... yes, it has been a long time ... '

After a quick exchange of pleasantries, Carla said, 'Can I ask you a quick question? Who's the best orthopaedic surgeon dealing with fractures in Morocco?'

Jilly paused. 'Have you broken something?'

No, it isn't for me. It's for a compound leg fracture ... a friend ... I'll explain later.'

'Why Morocco? You'd be far better off in England ...'

'I understand that, but I'm in Essaouira at the moment, and this friend is a Moroccan national. Too much red tape. If I could get to see someone while I'm here, it would be brilliant.'

'I see. I'll have to come back to you, Carla.'

Half an hour later, Jilly called back. 'It's a Mr Hussain. I'll send you his details. Is your email still the same...?'

Two days later, she managed to secure an appointment to see the surgeon at the hospital, and then only because she'd greased the palms of several personnel in the pecking order leading up to him.

'What you are asking is if I can perform another miracle. I re-examined the x-rays before you came in.' Leaning further over the desk, he clasped his hands together and said, 'I saved his leg, that was as much as I could do. This proposal ... I could re-operate ... I've been working closely with a colleague, a specialist in pioneering orthopaedic techniques. It *is* possible we can improve it ... maybe two more operations, but it will cost much money. Who will pay for this?'

'I will,' she said.

With a look of surprise, he scrawled a figure onto his pad and pushed it to her. 'You have this much money?'

Carla's took in the figure, her shock registering only in the tiniest flicker of her eyes. 'Yes,' she said, evenly. 'I'd like you to take all necessary steps to organize it, now. And the other thing is this ... I don't want anyone else to know. This is strictly between you and me. If anyone asks, you're to say that you believe the work was covered by an insurance payout. Do we have a deal?'

She put out her hand.

He took it. 'I'll get my secretary to organize the paperwork.'

Chapter 34

Essaouira, 15 February 2010

A little over two years had passed since Mohammed was summoned back to hospital for further consultations with Mr Hussain who had proposed, due to the nature of the fractures, the use of coral bone engineering.

Mohammed had endured a seemingly endless round of minor and not-so-minor operations. Third-generation implants were supplemented by pieces of bone harvested for reuse, for grafting and rebuilding the breaks in his leg. Plates were inserted, then wires and screws; he'd given up trying to keep track. The amount of bone needed meant a donor was required and, without hesitation, his father had volunteered grafts from his own hips and ribs.

Time dragged.

Finally, Mr Hussain had given permission for the cast to come off.

Mohammed had convalesced and waited, knowing that if he tried walking too soon he ran the risk of undoing all the good work.

At first he'd walked slowly, favouring the newly healed leg, afraid to put more weight on it. He followed a strict exercise regime, gradually rebuilding his physical strength. At times, when pushing himself too hard, he'd hear Mr Hussain's voice reminding him: *Don't rush things ...*

It was a beautiful spring morning; the sun blazed low in a cloudless, cerulean sky. He sat in the front seat of the car while his father drove his younger siblings to school and then, after that, they continued together into town.

'We will walk to the market for fish, for dinner tonight.'

Mohammed nodded. He felt giddy and lightheaded as if he could have walked for miles, if he'd wanted to. The cacophonous screeching of seagulls cheered him; to be so close to them once again ...

Strolling through the stone temple archway onto the harbour, he saw a group of his friends playing football. They saw him immediately and, calling his name, rushed to greet him.

Boomph. Someone kicked a ball and simultaneously shouted, 'Hey Mo ...'

Mohammed stepped two short paces and, half-turning, thrust his chest out to meet the ball. He stopped it. The ball dropped to his feet.

His foot rested on top and his eyes grew fierce, ready for the challenge.

'Be careful,' his father said. 'Your leg ...'

One of the boys cried, 'Mohammed ... Go!'

And he went – fleet, almost as before.

His father watched with pride as his son cut a swathe through the other boys, amid whoops of delight.

Leaning against a wall, he watched, thinking on their unknown benefactor; for he was no fool – there was no insurance. Could it have been the woman? The one Mohammed called 'lady'? No, he decided, she had already given money. If it had been her, she would have said.

He turned and gazed out over the gently bobbing blue vessels, and beyond ... across the sea and on to the horizon, where azure skies dipped and melded with the water in a misty heat-haze.

His thoughts touched on the boy's mother, his beloved wife, whom Allah had seen fit to take away from him. Overcome with emotion, he raised his voice, cracked and broken, unheard against the noise of screaming gulls ... realizing that while He takes with one hand, he gives with the other, he dropped his voice to a reverential whisper. '*Mon garçon miracle* ... Allah be praised.'

ABOUT THE AUTHOR

Max currently works as a construction professional, writing in his spare time. His debut novel *The Sister*, was released in November 2013.
The Life and Times of William Boule, is his second novel.

Max China is a pen name.

www.ingramcontent.com/pod-product-compliance
Lightning Source LLC
Chambersburg PA
CBHW071250130626
46556CB00003B/1242